Latins Anonymous

Two Plays

Arte Público Press
Houston, Texas
1996

rough grants from the
a federal agency), Andrew
Wallace-Reader's Digest
l of Houston.

Recovering the past, creating the future

Arte Público Press
University of Houston
Houston, Texas 77204-2090

Cover design by Mark Pinón

Latins anonymous / by Latins Anonymous.
        p.   cm.
Written by Luisa Leschin ... [et al.].
ISBN 1-55885-172-0 (trade pbk. : alk. paper)
1. American drama—Hispanic American
authors. 2. American drama—20th century.
3. Hispanic Americans—Drama. 4. American
drama (Comedy) I. Leschin, Luisa. II. Latins
Anonymous.
PS628.H57L38   1996
812'.5408086872—dc20   96-26649
                                    CIP

Contents

Introduction by Edward James Olmos

Before the Latino comedy group Latins Anonymous burst onto the theatrical scene in 1987, little Latino sketch comedy could be found in our ancient land of Aztlán. Luis Valdez and El Teatro Campesino published *Actos,* their raw, satirical, agitprop playlets over a decade before. These *Actos,* which had influenced a generation of Latino actors, dealt with the birth of *Chicanismo* and the plight of the farm worker. But who was going to speak to this new generation, which included sophisticated, mainstream, multi-national, urban dwellers whose American experience was more complex than that of their parents? Hence the birth of Latins Anonymous, whose sharp insight into the foibles of the vast immigrant experience brought a rare brand of irreverence, energy and confidence to the new American theatre scene.

When I first participated in Luis Valdez' masterpiece *Zoot Suit,* at the Music Center of Los Angeles during the late '70's, we hoped it would herald a new beginning of Chicano theatre. But it has been too slow in coming. So when Latins Anonymous, the first of several such improvisational comedy groups, broke into our consciousness, their voices were strongly welcomed. At last, here was a group which addressed the unique, beautiful, sometimes mind-bending duality of the Latino/a living in *el norte!* The actors/writers themselves hailed from México, Colombia, Guatemala and the American Southwest, and their work revealed the hidden cadences of English, *español, caló,* and Spanglish.

Moreover, this new generation of comic performers integrated hard-edged "Saturday Night Live" sketch comedy with the fundamentals of *teatro,* which was based on the Mexican vaudeville *tanda* and honed on the backroad farmlands of Central California, Arizona and Texas. They created an amalgam which was truly their own by mixing the *ganas* (guts) and purpose of *teatro* with the slickness of American sketch comedy.

The 1980's had promised to be the "Decade of the Latino," but by the time Latins Anonymous arrived on the scene, the young group had to address why *la comunidad* was barely recognizing its political clout and still hadn't seized its economic power. We didn't understand why Latinos were still perceived as "anonymous" in the broader U.S. society. Even those who had become Yuppie Mexicans, or "yupsicans," were still seeking normalcy while battling the prevailing racism. These facts had a profound impact on the artists who made up the first company of Latins Anonymous - Luisa Leschin, Armando Molina, Rick Nájera and Diane Rodríguez - and inspired them to write the first of their two plays, "Latins Anonymous."

"Latins Anonymous" was a comedic analysis of the contemporary Latino condition, featuring a series of playlets tackling such maladies as how nationalism keeps us divided ("Las Comadres"), terminal machismo ("Machos of Omaha") and those who deny their roots by referring to themselves as European ("Latin Denial"). The show became an instant critical and commercial success, first at the Los Angeles Theatre Center and then in San Diego. It was embraced because our audiences had never seen their neurosis portrayed so accurately and with such hilarious results! Was it any wonder it became the most produced Latino comedy in the country?

Three years later, the group was joined by comedian Cris Franco and went on to bite the hand that fed it by creating "The La La Awards," a scathing indictment of the Latinos' ever-precarious relationship with Hollywood. It had become painfully clear to all that Latinos were too hip for the Hollywood Room. Outraged that the '80's had come and gone and most Latinos were still relegated to stereotypical roles, "The La La Awards" asked why negative media representations continued to impact our reality. This environmental play expressed our struggle not only as citizens, but as artists as well.

Critics recognized the underlying seriousness behind the comedy when they said, "this show knows what ails Latinos and prescribes comedy as its "medicine" and "it hits a comedic bullseye" because the show successfully attacked the icons attributed to us: the self-martyring Latin Spitfire, the perennial gangbanger, the Latin lover with his brains in his pants, and such celebrities at St. Edward James Almost ...¡Dios mío! No one was spared as "The La La Awards" went on to many successful Los Angeles runs and a long tour of the Southwest.

To see an original performance of a Latins Anonymous show was an event. In addition to the talents of these fine actors/writers, they brought together renowned artists to enhance and punctuate their message. The creative team of "The La La Awards" reads like a veritable Who's Who in the Los Angeles art scene, employing the talents of visual artists such as Gronk who designed the scenery, and Patssi Valdez who carefully crafted thoughtfully outrageous and character - defining costumes.

Hermanos y hermanas, it is wonderful to know that through the publishing of these plays, future generations of readers, performers, scholars and critics will be exposed to material specific to our experiences. You are holding in your hands a tribute to tenacity, courage, intelligence and self-belief; a realization that audiences can be trusted to listen, to believe, and to laugh. May we continue to express our *alma y corazón.* Let la raza be anonymous no more! *Paz.*

Acknowledgements:

Latins Anonymous wish to thank the following individuals for their support, dedication and generosity of spirit:

Doña Adler and Giles Bateman, Eddie Ayala, Fausto Bara, Jim Billings, Bill Bushnell, Alina Cenal, Rose Cano, Rosalie Portillo and Gemma Sandoval of Plaza de la Raza, Elsbeth Collins, Casey Coss, Scott Forbes and Mark Gallo and the old Backlot Staff, Tony Frankel, Maria Elena Gaitan and her son, Octavio Gaitan, Felipe Galvez, Leo Garcia, Marie Paul Goislard, Ron Goswick, Dan Guerrero, Lalo Guerrero, Robecca Gonzalez-Harrier, Ginger Holguin, Andy Howard, Lisa Loomer, Dara Marks, Jeff Murray and Nicolette Chaffey of Theater Theatre, Angela Najera, Evangeline Ordaz, Olga Perez, Rick Perkins, Miguel Angel Reyes, Dale Reynolds, Andy and Irene Robinson, Vance Sanders, Jack Scalici, Jerry Sickler, Michael Seel and Ando Iovino, Andrea and Jody Simon, David Smoot, Adrian Tafoya, Louis A. Vrabel, Mike Wise, Diane White, Sam Woodhouse and Doug Jacobs of San Diego Repertory, Carmen Zapata, Estela Escarlata and Margarita Galvan of the Bilingual Foundation of the Arts, Joan Foster, Susie Virgilio, Keoni, Julie Page, John Gibson, Jeff Stafford, Amber Winner, Peter Clines, Tim McGuire and all the "dudes" at San Diego Rep.

And most of all, to the memory of our friends, Mr. Robert Vega, Mr. Ed Najera and Mr. Juan Carlos Nagel.

Latins Anonymous

Two Plays

The
LA LA Awards

by

Cris Franco
Luisa Leschin
Armando Molina
Diane Rodríguez

"The LA LA Awards" *is a satirical, up-to-the minute look at the Latino presence in Hollywood. All characters are broad versions of their obvious counterparts and should be played with* ganas *and love. Jokes and references should be updated whenever possible. This script is dedicated to all those wonderful icons whose talent, hard work and dedication have given us something to parody.*

🔲🔲🔲

The very glamorous "LA LA Awards" *premiered at the Japan American Theatre in Little Tokyo, Los Angeles, on October 8, 1992, with the following cast:*

Cris Franco as Protester, Chicklat Dancer, Mr. Mexico, Mr. Old El Paso Salsa, Mr. Free Trade Agreement, Running Jaw, Edward James Almost, Oscar de la Hoya, Maclovio Mojado, La Twinkles, Los Globos singer, Linda Roncha's guitarist, Barry *and* Juan José "The Gang- Banger" Valentino Jiménez.

Luisa Leschin as Protester, Chicklat Dancer, Miss Puerto Rico, Miss Taco Shell, Cortez, Roseanne Barrio, Los Globos singer, Linda Roncha, Meryl Estripada/Mrs. Wright *and* Wendy.

Armando Molina as Protester, Moctezuma, Cheech Marin County, Juan Valdez, Rudy, Antonio Nalgueras *and* Fea.

Diane Rodriguez as Protester, Chicklat Dancer, Miss Cuba, Miss Bilingual U.S.A., Miss Hispanic Market, Miss Media Statistics, Malinche, Churro, Los Globos singer, Mary Qué, María *and* Sad Girl.

Supporting cast members included: Liz González, Martín Hernández, Demetrius Navarro, Erica Ortega, Gabriel Roland, Paul G. Saucido, Luis Villalta, Anne Marie Williams and José Delgado as the Announcer.

José Luis Valenzuela	Director
Miguel Delgado	Choreographer
Jose Lopez	Lighting Designer
Gronk / Steve La Ponsie	Set Designer
Patssi Valdez	Costume Designer
Joseph Julian Gonzalez	Composer & Arranger
Mark Friedman	Sound Designer
Joe Romano	Additional Music
Ilene Poff	Prop Designer

THE LA LA AWARDS continued its sparkling cavalcade of ethnic excess in January, 1993 at The San Diego Repertory. Produced by Sam Woodhouse, it featured the original cast with the following ensemble:

Evangeline Fernandez, Calixto Hernandez, Definique Juniel, Dewain Robinson, Jaime Rodriguez, and Julia Romero

The Set

A giant eight-foot likeness of the LA LA Award (a statue wrapped in gold mylar and bound with gold chord) stands stage right. A glitzy podium, inside which many of the props are hidden, stands stage left. Giant wood cutouts of glittery "cactus" flank the stage left and right wings. Centered over the proscenium hangs a round, large, Mayan-meets-Hollywood rendering of the comedy and tragedy masks.

The action is continuous and takes place on-stage at the LA LA Awards Ceremony in Heartbreak City, a.k.a. Hollywood, California.

¿Es ésta su imagen?
Is This Your Image?

The theatre's lobby is decorated with giant blowups of the latest news clippings reporting the recent immigrant bashing, gang warfare, pregnant teen Latina statistics, etc. Amidst the cultural collage stands a full-length mirror with the message written, "¿Es ésta su imagen?" and "Is this your image?"

A television monitor shows a time capsule of the history of Latinos on film. It is a series of quick crosscuts featuring such characters as Pepino from "The Real McCoys," Marlon Brando as "Zapata," Robby Benson as a cholo in "Gangs," Marissa Tomei in "The Perez Family," mixed with the latest news telecasts as well as footage of Cheech and Chong getting loaded driving in their low rider in "Up in Smoke," Charo, gang girls talking about sex in "My Vida Loca," Argentine soccer players eating each other in "Alive!" and Antonio Banderas blowing away greasy bandits in "Desperado."

Preshow—The Protesters

At 20 minutes to curtain: Outside the theater The Protesters *urge the arriving attendees to boycott tonight's LA LA Awards Show, claiming it perpetuates the stereotyping and exploitation of Latinos in the media. They carry protest signs, some reading: Honk If You're Honduran, The LA LA Awards Perpetuate Latino Stereotypes, Latinos We Need Ya, We've Got to Stop the Media, All Latinos Aren't Maids, Gang-Bangers and Prostitutes, I'm Getting Mayan Act Together and Aztec'n It on the Road!, Free Freddy Fender!*

PROTESTERS: (*They chant.*)
> Get tough, don't panic. We're Latino not Hispanic!
> Latinos, we need ya, we've got to stop the media.
> Be smart, now's the hour, time to show your pocho power!

I love my home, I love my raza, but not the TV in my
    casa!

*At 10 minutes to curtain: Forcing themselves into the the-
ater lobby,* The Protesters *shout that the audience members
must be aware that they will be seeing stereotypes on stage.
They argue loudly.*

PROTESTERS: (*Randomly exclaiming.*)
    Not all Cubans speak fast.
    Not all Salvadorians are illegal.
    Not all Peruvian Presidents are Japanese.
    Not all Puerto Ricans are on welfare.
    Some Mexican's have auto insurance.
    You're going to see Latinos playing gang members and
        maids.
    You'll see women in braids, guys in sombreros and people
        with moustaches...some of them men.

At 8 minutes to curtain: The House Manager *and a* Few
Ushers *escort* The Protesters *out of the house and back onto
the street, explaining that the theatre patrons deserve the right
to make up their own minds. The* Theater Manager *threatens
to have the* Police/Security *remove them by force. An alterca-
tion almost occurs but* The Protesters *back down and exit
chanting.*

K-TAL Radio

*Upon entering the theatre the audience listens to a ten-
minute tape, an audio-montage sounding as if someone is
quickly flipping through Spanish and English radio and TV
stations. Sound bytes of our media past, including Desi Arnaz,
Gloria Estefan, "West Side Story" and Speedy Gonzales, all
flip through the airwaves and finally fade away.*

Cold open, house lights down.

Oye como va

ANNOUNCER: Welcome, *damas y caballeros*. Tonight's LA LA Awards are being broadcast via satellite to 25,000,000 Latinos in Aztechnicolor and Lopezsound... "¡Oye como va!" (*We hear the "THX" chord swell into El Chicano's "Oye como va" translation: Get into the vibes. A slide is projected a la "THX": Lopez Sound..."Oye como va." Drum roll into opening number.*) And to start our phantasmagoria of ethnic excess, the Chicano-Latino "chicklat" dancers. (*The Chicklat Dancers enter and flail their bodies to the salsa rhythms of the opening theme. Dressed only in spangles and tights, they leap about the stage with little regard for the laws of taste or decorum. Screaming typical Spanish expressions of excitement, such as "andale" and "arriba," the trio throw their bodies beneath the giant LA LA Award statue stage right, finally ending their dance/ ritual by kneeling and worshipping it with pagan abandon, as if it were a golden calf. They are awakened from their gyrating trance-like state by the introduction of the first host.*) And now, ladies and gentlemen, introducing one of the most successful Latinos in the history of entertainment...star of film, television and eight-track...you see him weekly in his hit series *Hash Bridges*...Mr. Cheech Marin County!

Cheech Marin County

The Chicklat Dancers *quickly exit, giving* Cheech *the "high five." Wearing a tuxedo and an American-flag headband, a long-haired, mustached, burned-out hippie-type in his late forties,* Cheech Marin County *steps up to the podium with a king-size reefer in hand.*

CHEECH: (*Sounding a little stoned.*) Wow, man! *Orale,* what's happening? I'm Cheech Marin County. To all my *amigos,* "*buenas noches,*" and to all you surfer-types, "bogus nachos."

With so many awards shows like the Grammy's, the Tony's, the Chuey's, we thought we'd award ourselves. So welcome to "ta-da..." (*Indicate the statue.*) The Los Angeles Lifetime Achievement Awards, or "The LA LA Awards"...not to be confused with the Cuban American Community Awards or the "CA CA Awards." First joke the white folks won't get.

How many Latinos in the house tonight? Wow! The whole casts of "Mi Familia," "Selena," and "Evita" are here. Is there anyone here who doesn't speak any Spanish? (*If someone raises his hand, speak directly to him or her. If no one raises a hand, confront someone who looks like they can handle a little audience abuse.*) And you paid full price? Okay, we gotta help you out, that dude/dudette next to you, he/she will be your translator. Just know that when we're all laughing and having fun...we're laughing at you. And there'll be a lot to laugh at because tonight we honor all those Latino-Chicano-Hispanics who have achieved the heights of visibility and the pinnacles of success in all fields—particularly in the fields of Fresno and Bakersfield ("*Or your local field.*").

It's really exciting backstage, every Latino star is here...all five of them. You will be seeing greats, near greats and people who are just grateful to be alive and working in Hollywood, which is Spanish for "Latinos need not apply."

And we owe this success and our stellar image to those fabulous film classics: "Tony and the Greaser," "The Greaser's Revenge" and "Die Greasier." And not only in

films; we're getting a lot of visibility today. We're everywhere, every off-ramp, every yard... (*Poses like the "alien
crossing" sign.*) crossing every highway. So put on your
Galavision glasses and let *el show* begin.

And to celebrate our role as the snag in the fabric of
American society, here are the Chicano-Latino or Chicklat Dancers in our salute to the International Moment of
the Latino. Maestro? Tape!

The International Moment of the Latino

SFX: Music. The Chicklat Dancers *enter with much attitude, wearing banners reading: LA LA Awards.*

CHEECH: Miss Puerto Rico!

MISS PUERTO RICO: (*Heavy Puerto Rican accent.*) I'm from
the capital of Puerto Rico: Manhattan.

CHEECH: Miss Cuba.

MISS CUBA: (*Heavy Cuban-American accent.*) I'm from the
capital of Cuba...Miami.

CHEECH: Mr. Mexico.

MR. MEXICO: I'm from the capital of Mexico...Los Angeles,
California. (*They parade off-stage waving and blowing
kisses to the adoring audience.*)

CHEECH: There they are, ladies and gentlemen, Latin America's greatest export: it's people! That's the international
picture. Moving closer to home, let's welcome our local
beauties! (Cheech *leads the audience in giving a big hand
to the same trio. Still waving and blowing kisses, they
return to the stage wearing the same outfits and fake
smiles.*) Aren't they lovely! Miss Taco Shell!

MISS TACO SHELL: They love our food, but they can't stom-
ach us.

CHEECH: Make a run for the border! Miss Bilingual U.S.A.!

MISS BILINGUAL USA: I live in Los Angeles, drive a Fiesta, work on La Cienega, eat Loco Pollo and drink margaritas. Why are we so afraid of Spanish? We speak it already.

CHEECH: Can we say, "¿Dónde esta la biblioteca?" Mr. Old El Paso Salsa!

MR. OLD EL PASO SALSA: (*With a western twang.*) Salsa's now the most eaten condiment in the United States. And remember, if you want safe snacks, use a condiment.

CHEECH: Preferably, fiesta colored! Miss Hispanic Market!

MISS HISPANIC MARKET: With a buying power of over five billion dollars, you think they'd try to sell us something!

CHEECH: And that's a lot of *churros*. Mister Free Trade Agreement.

MR. FREE TRADE AGREEMENT: It's the good neighbor policy. America gains jobs by sending them south, Mexico makes money by selling themselves cheap. Makes sense to me!

CHEECH: What did he say? I gotta take Remedial NAFTA 101. Here's Miss Media Statistics!

MISS MEDIA STATISTICS: The *L.A. Times* states that there are more extraterrestrials and dinosaurs appearing on television than there are Latinos.

CHEECH: Hey, we've got dinosaurs... Haven't you heard of a Barriosaures-Mex? And our final contestant, Mr. Latino Voter! (*No one enters.*) Ms. Latino Voter? (*No one enters.*) Mr. Latino Voter doesn't appear to be with us. Maybe he thinks there's too many of us to fit into a voting booth. I vote we go to a commercial. (*All exit. Crossfade to ...*)

Chican O's

Oscar de la Hoya *shadow boxing in trunks, gloves, and olympic medal dangling around his neck. Near him is a table with a large box of cereal, with the front turned upstage, a*

*large spoon and a container filled with guacamole (It can be
cottage cheese mixed with green food coloring.)*

    ANNOUNCER: Hey, Olympic Gold Medalist Oscar
de la Hoya, what's your favorite breakfast cereal?
*(Carlos shadowboxes over to the table, flashes a toothy
grin, picks up the cereal box and turns it around. It says:
"Chican O's Cereal.")* Right! CHICAN O'S! *(Quickly pours
a lot of cereal into the bowl.)* The breakfast of Mexicans.
Little brown toasted CHICAN O'S taste great with milk
or guacamole! *(Quickly pours guacamole over the cereal.)*
CHICAN O'S! *(He joyously eats a mouthful of the awful
stuff. Blackout.)*

Cheech Continued

CHEECH: *(Returning.)* Personally, I like Cholo Charms. You
    know, "Pink Chevy's, green cards, yellow spray cans.
    They're Hispanically delicious!" And now the awards. For
    our first category, Best Latino Game Show. And the nomi-
    nees are: "The Ten Trillion Peso Pyramid," that's like four
    bucks, "The Price is Right On"...if it's at Pic'NSave. And
    "Wheel of Fresno" *(Or your local city everyone wants to
    leave.).* I guess the winner gets to leave. But the winner is
    "The Aztec Dating Game"...the game where we find new
    love in the new world. And now for a live re-enactment
    clip...*(He exits also ...)*

Aztec Studs

Slides of the bloody conquest of Mexico are projected as
Running Jaw, *a fast-talking game-show host, enters. He wears
a bright up-scale three-piece suit and small headdress. He*

bangs a traditional Aztec drum to punctuate jokes and to get the crowd excited.

RUNNING JAW: Moyolo-chocoyotzin-tlateo-matini! That's Nahuatl for "Hi, warriors and virgins." I'm your host, Running Jaw, and welcome to Meso-America's number one game show...Aztec Studs.

It's time to meet our first Azetc Stud. He is a graduate of the Institute of Aztecnology, where he majored in irrigation so he dates primarily during the dry season. He's ruler absolute, direct descendant of our Sun God, Quetzalcoatl, and a great guy. Let's all say Moyolo-chocoyotzin-tlateo-matini and give a great big Aztec Studs welcome to...Moctezuma! (Moctezuma, *leader of the Aztecs, enters decked out in giant headdress, holding a blood-stained machete. Running Jaw drops to his knees before him.*)

MOCTEZUMA: (*To* Running Jaw.) You may live.

RUNNING JAW: "Mocte," why don't you tell the tribe a little about yourself?

MOCTEZUMA: My turn-ons are older women, eleven and over. And my turn-offs are vengeful gods. (*Waving a fist the at air.*) Why I ought to...

RUNNING JAW: Are you pumped for the game?

MOCTEZUMA: Well, I'm having a bad-feather day, but aside from that... (*Gives the okay sign.*)

RUNNING JAW: Our next stud hails from the Old World, *España*. He enjoys traveling, meeting new people and conquering them. Let's all say Moyolo-chocowatza-Boom chucka-boom-chuck-lucka to Hernando Cortez! (*Cortez enters wearing full conquistador armor and bulging codpiece.*)

RUNNING JAW: Yo, Hernando!

CORTEZ: (*Lisping heavily.*) ¡Saludoth! *Eth un gran plather, esthar aqui con uthtedes esta noche.*

RUNNING JAW: Thuffering Thucotash! Now let's meet our three lovely virgins. Here are Fertile Frog, Passion Lizard and that Berlitz beauty who is about to sell her people down the river, Malinche! (*Only* Malinche, *a budding Aztec babe, enters.*) Where are the other girls?

MALINCHE: Bummer, they got sacrificed.

RUNNING JAW: The Gods must be crazy! You all know how we play the game. Our contestants have all gone out with each other. Whoever gets the most questions right about their "get-to-know-you" date, marries Malinche, wins cash prizes and gets to rule the Americas! Gents, you all pumped for the game?

ALL: Yeah!

CORTEZ: *¡Theguro!*

RUNNING JAW: Who was Malinche talking about when she said, "He had dried snake's breath."

MOCTEZUMA: Guilty. That's gotta be me.

RUNNING JAW: (*Tossing a bloody "heart."*) Correctamundo, you win a human heart.

MOCTEZUMA: Not expecting a romantic interlude, I forgot my Toltec Tic-Tacs.

MALINCHE: Romance? There wasn't much chemistry...there wasn't even astronomy. I wasn't impressed with how he planned the date. We climbed 539 steps up the Pyramid of the Sun, and the disco was closed, bummer!

MOCTEZUMA: It wasn't closed, it was "All-Mayan Night."

MALINCHE: Excuse me, I'm am *Aztec* Princess and I expect to be treated like one.

MOCTEZUMA: Well, eat my heart! I'm used to women who are into grinding and I'm not talking corn.

MALINCHE: Piss off, darky. This is a whole new world. I want a hairy guy with an exploding rod who isn't afraid of exploring uncharted virgin territory, namely me.

RUNNING JAW: Go on, Aztec-Indian girl!

MALINCHE: Face it, you're on the way out! (*Running Jaw leads audience into catcalls.*)

MOCTEZUMA: So 500 years of Aztec supremacy are ancient history because Spanish shorty here just bats his baby blues?

MALINCHE: That's right, something like that. You little dweeb! (Moctezuma *and* Malinche *start to arm wrestle, she quickly overcomes him, sending him to the floor.*)

RUNNING JAW: We've got tribal disunity, what a great game! But, let's move on to the next question. About whom was Malinche talking when she said, "He put the 'kiss' in 'conquistador.'"

CORTEZ: Running Jawbone, she's ethpeaking about me.

RUNNING JAW: (*Tossing* Cortez *a 'human heart.'*) That's right! And the game is tied.

CORTEZ: Ick! Well, "R.J.," she was some hot Aztec love kitten. (*The rest of the cast pull out bags of popcorn, with ears of corn still sticking out, and loudly munch as* Cortez *launches into a Tony Award-winning soliloquy.*) I came to to the New World to conquer the Aztec Empire, but instead, Malinche, that Tempting Translator, conquered me. Oh! The *señorita* gives great headdress. Let me tell thee, life at sea is no picnic. Sure my cabin boy looks great in garters and a wig, and does a great Dolores Del Río impression... but nothing compares with the real thing. Alack, I am fortune's fool and Malinche's, too! Ohhhhhhhh!

RUNNING JAW: (*All return to their places, as* Running Jaw *leads the audience in applause.*) Wow, that was better than "El Cid." Let's hear it for the spic, folks. Is that a great story or what? So, Malinche, did he plant his flag and claim you for Spain?

MALINCHE: R.J., I never knew I was into white men until I saw him. He was hung like a horse, then he got off his horse. So I just flicked my fabulous *greñas* to reveal my "chichimecas" and said, "Moyolo chocoyotzin tlateo matini," that's Nahuatl for "'Allo love.' Let's play Magellan, you circumnavigate my globes and I'll prove the world's not flat!"

CORTEZ: Oh! Throbbing loins! Come with me, darling, I'll give you everything! Syphilis. Smallpox. Uptight Catholic kids and a lifetime of servitude.

MOCTEZUMA: No, come with me! I'll give you tribal disunity, bloody sacrifices, short, dark, flat-nosed kids and paintings of Elvis on black velvet.

MALINCHE: (*Directing* Cortez *to kill* Moctezuma.) Kill 'im! (*A fight ensues,* Moctezuma *whips out his machete, does some fancy sword work.* Cortez *takes out his musket and fires at* Moctezuma, *mortally wounding him.*)

MOCTEZUMA: (*SFX: thunder and lightning throughout.*) You'll pay for this. (*To audience.*) You're *all* gonna pay for this. *Hamana, hamana!* (*Does a Gleason death.*) I'm gonna curse you from here to 1999. Your names will be mispronounced for five-hundred years. You'll work really hard, but everyone will think you're lazy. You're gonna live in the City of Angels, but it's gonna be hell, and you and all your half-breed Mestizo brats will be cursed with anonymity until the year 2000. That's two (*He clutches his heart and sways back and forth in pain.*) -oh-oh-oh. (*He falls silent to the floor... then sits up.*) And you, Hernando Cortez, I have *one* word for you: *Generalísimo* Franco. (*He dies.*)

RUNNING JAW: Wow, the curse of Moctezuma. Heavy stuff. But that means you two win! And all you out there can watch our new *telenovela*, "Moctezuma's Revenge." We think it's gonna run about 500 years. Let's say good-bye. (*They blow the audience a "Dating Game" type kiss.*) Moyolochocoyotzin Tlateo Matini. We'll see you all in the New World! (*They exit as lights cross fade to ...*)

ANNOUNCER: And now, ladies and gentlemen, the king of *carnales*, the prince of pachucos! Saint Edward James Almost!

Edward James Almost

Edward James Almost as he stalks panther-like onto the stage, dressed in black zoot suit and matching hat.

EDWARD: *Gracias, raza.* I'm Edward James Almost and I can do this! (*Taking a backbreaking "pachuco" stance.*) *¡Orale!* You are all very honored to have me here tonight. I'm the busiest Chicano icon in Hollywood. I'm not only a singer, actor, writer, dancer, producer, breath mint, candy mint, cultural spokesman and all-purpose Chicano demigod... I'm now also director of my own all-Latino classical ensemble called the Chicano American Repertory with Acting Shakespearean Hispanics...or "C.A.R.W.A.S.H." *¡Orale!* This year C.A.R.W.A.S.H. is proud to present our all-Chicano production of Guillermo Shakespeare's greatest tragedy, *Romeo and Juliet*, re-titled *Romeo y Julietta*. Significantly rewritten and updated, this production allows we Chicanos to break out of our stereotypical roles as hoodlums and gang-bangers who are always killing each other...to playing classical hoodlums and gangbangers who are always killing each other. *Simón, ese.* And if you see *el show*, you'll see me, 'cause I'm in it. *Pues, sí.* In Act "I" (*Eye.*), I play a Montague, and in Act "II" (*Eye-eye.*)...I play an autoworker. So come on down to the Montebello Center for Performing and Martial Arts and see *Romeo y Julietta*; forsooth *y órale!*

Enough about American me. I'm here to introduce a very important *ruca* who raised herself up from the barrio... She's an "*a toda madre-ruca-carnala-de-aquellas.*" Look it up. A woman who combines bleach with brains. An Oil of Olay recipient. Let's give a great big Edward James Almost *Orale* to Miss Mary Qué, *órale!*

Mary Qué

Mary Qué, a decadent-type woman enters wearing dark glamour glasses, donning a Marilyn Monroe wig and speaking with a breathy southern accent.

MARY: (*Licking her lips.*) Mmm! Mr. "Stand and Deliver." Edward honey, sometime why don't you and I lay down and deliver. Ooo! Who would have thought that little ol' me from South Pico Rivera (*Or any local Latino community.*), born to a poor Mexican family, would have turned Mary Qué Cosmetics into a million-dollar empire for the facially handicapped. Oil of Ole! I can't believe I'm receiving a lifetime achievement award and I'm only 25-years old. It's unbelievable!

   I personally want to thank the LA LA board members, whom I happen to have given personal make overs to all night long. It was exhausting!

   Do you want to look like any of the stars you see here tonight or on "Siempre en Domingo?" Well, I can turn anyone into a cover girl or boy if you just use Mary Qué Cosmetics or become a Mary Qué distributor and win yourself a Pink Pinto. I started out small by making over my mother's side of the family. For example: (*Slide of a rugged looking "India"—Mexican-Indian woman.*) My aunt Malinche Guadalupe Gómez came in and needed help. She had just been through a messy divorce and needed a lift. So I said, "Tía, I'm calling you 'Michelle' 'cause your name's too hard for me to pronounce. She, like everyone on my mother's side of the family, had a flat face like a tortilla, dark illegal brown skin and a body like a tamale. I, of course, have worked on mine. So I did a little contouring and the results... (*Slide of Cher.*) Doesn't she look beautiful? Fifty-years old! It's unbelievable! (*Slide of Guatemalan-Indian woman.*)

Now my cousin came in and had a problem with her hair. (*Slide of woman with straight, stringy hair.*) It was straight and shiny. It had no body. Disgusting! I of course had hair like this and I knew exactly what to do. I processed it and gave her... (*Slide of horrifyingly plastic Loni Anderson.*) ...the "Loni Anderson Mall" look! She loves her new look and begs for more.

Now this woman came in, poor thing, horrible thick eyebrows and a moustache. Now, women, moustaches are not a problem. With my special technique it doesn't hurt a bit. I just pluck them out hair by hair and the results...I turned this woman... (*Slide of Frida Kahlo.*) ...into this woman... (*Slide of Madonna.*)

I care about selling you beauty, so your dreams will come true. American Dream—I can make it happen. (*Breathily singing, a la Marilyn Monroe.*) "Happy birthday, Mary Qué Cosmetics. Happy birthday to me..." (*Lights slowly out as she sings. Then ...*)

Slide: Pocha—a Chicana who gets a C- in Spanish.

ANNOUNCER: The winner of Best Pocha singer of the year is...Miss Linda Roncha.

Slide: "Canciones de Mi Padre" album cover.

Linda Roncha

Lights come up on a tableu vivant, a recreation of Linda Ronstadt's album cover, "Canciones de mi padre." The music from "La Cigarra" is playing. Linda Roncha *and her* Guitarist *are costumed in industrial-strength folkloric attire. She breaks out of the tableau and sings.*

Note: Throughout this entire sketch, the Guitarist *will often plead, cajole and demand that the audience applaud for our recording superstar.*

LINDA: (*Singing to the tune of "La Cigarra."*)
    My nombre's Linda Roncha
    Mexicanos like me a buncha

    Holding notes are my forte
    So I do it all over *el norte.*

    The ranchera fills my soul! (*She holds note.*)
    Chihuahua, what breath control.

    Look at the bows in my hair,
    As ethnic as I can be.
    Spangles down to there,
    Like a piñata threw up on me!
    I could inflate a zeppelin
    with my lung capacity!

    I'll hold this note! (*Holds note 4 bars while drinking a trick glass of water.*)

    I'll hold this note! (*Music goes up a third. She throws herself to the ground and holds the note 8 bars while doing one-armed push-ups.*)

    This one could hurt! (*Music goes up one step. The* Guitarist *brings on a trick sword and hands it to* Linda. *She stands and holds the note 10 bars while swallowing the sword.*)

    Money makers, money makers,
    My albums sells like tortillas.

    I'm no folkloric-faker;
    More Mexican than Pancho Villa.

    I'm donating my vocal chords to the Smithsonian,
    You get the idea.

    Listen to this thiiiiiiii… (*The music vamps and we fade from her real voice into a looped tape of her holding the same note. She is assisted by the* Guitarist *in a series of rapid-fire cartoon-style comic bits to show the passing of time. The* Guitarist *brings on a magic table and hands her a magic hat and wand.* Linda *shows the audience the hat is empty. She taps it twice and pulls out flowers. She taps the hat again and pulls out a string of colored scarves. The* Guitarist *brings on a small oven, large mixing bowl with flour in it and a big wooden mixing spoon.* Linda *ethnically dances over to the oven. She starts mixing the contents of the bowl, offers the* Guitarist *a taste, he likes it. He opens the oven door, she places the bowl into the trick oven and shuts the door. SFX: An oven timer bell goes off. They both lick their chops as from the oven they pull out a tall "pasteleria"-type cake.* Linda *pretends to lick the frosting but starts to get stomach cramps. Confused, the* Guitarist *brings on a stool. She no sooner sits down when she starts going into labor. The* Guitarist *guides her in Lamaze breathing exercises and the cramps get more severe. He cautiously digs underneath her layers of petticoats to pull out a little baby girl with big braids in her hair. He holds the baby doll,* Linda *kisses her, then he throws the baby offstage.* Linda *gets angry, chases him around the stage and corners him, but she's running out of breath. She stops, reaches into the* Guitarist's *trousers and pulls out his boxer shorts with the red-hearts pattern.)* ...iiii-iiiiiiiiiiiiis!

(*Singing.*) Los calzones de mi padre!

GUITARIST: ¡Ay, ay!

Blackout

Churro

ANNOUNCER: Please welcome a woman whose lips know no rest...the inevitable Churro!

An explosion of blonde hair, thick lips and thicker accent, Churro *shakes her fabulous bod like a nine-point quake whenever she shouts her trademark "¡ay, ay, ay!"*

CHURRO: *¡Ay! ¡Ay! ¡Ay, ay, ay!* Isn't tonight fantastic! It's so beautiful to see we Latinos working together to create this beautiful event! *¡Ay, ay, ay!* Everything's too fancy and so shmancy. The age of the Latino is here! "The Sleeping Giant" is waking up and I'm the alarm clock! *¡Ay, ay, ay!*

You're going to be so proud of my English. *Grathias, grathias,* I amg Churro and I amg hippy to be here tonight. The LA LA Awards are my favorite because I can pronounce them.

Isn't it wonderful to be alive during the age of communication? These LA LA Awards are being washed by millionth y millionth of English and Espanich-speaking persongs, so tonight I amg being misunderstood in two languish. *¡Ay, ay!* My accent is not a put-on (*putón*), but my hair dresser is. *¡Ay, ay!*

It's so wonderful to be bilingüe. People are paranoid that when people espeak Espanish we are talking about themg. It's true!

I espeak persthonally three languishes: English, Spanish, Etalian y Yapanese...and they all esound the same. *¡Ay, ay, ay!* The best way to make friends is to tongue them in their own language. Everybody asks me, Churro, "Why can't Latino's lose their accent?" For one, I wouldn't have a career.

It is very important to communicate in at least two languages. Look at president Clinton, he espeaks double talk.

The nominees for the best weatherman are... Weathermen are so weird, they're the only people who are constantly wrong and still keep their jobs. The nominees are... Dallas Rains, Johnny Mountain, Storm Fields, Wet Dreams, Dry Heaves, and the winner is... Maclovio Mojado.

The Cultural Climate

Our white-washed weatherman, Maclovio Mojado, *enters wheeling in his large weather map. With the aid of his pointer and props, he reports on Latinos living in the U.S. and on the cultural climate in the regions particular to each nationality.* Churro *'Air Kisses'* Moclavio *and hands him an award.*

MACLOVIO: (*Heavy pocho accent.*) Much Grass, Churro. I never won anything before in my life. (Churro *breaks into an "Ay, ay ay" attack and throws her back out.* Maclovio *helps her limp off-stage.*)

Let's give a big hand to Churro. As we say in weather talk, there goes a big front.

¡Hola amigos! My name is Maclovio Mojado and I am the new breed of Latino; I am a Yuppie Mexican, or a Yupsican, and I'm here to report to you the cultural climate in these great *Estados Unidos.* As always, this segment will be brought to you by Spud and Spud Light. (*Hold up a can of 'Spud' and 'Spud Light.'*) Beer companies are the main sponsors of all Latino programming... because when you're high... (*Sticks 'Spud' can up north and 'Spud Light' can down south.*) ...you don't care about how low your wages are.

Let's take a look at el *mapa*...el *mapa*! All along the West Coast and in parts of the Southwest there is a sixty-five percent chance of Mexicans... (*Sticks little Mexican mariachi hat on Los Angeles.*) ...with scattered Salvadori-

ans. (*Sticks little green squirt-gun near San Diego.*) *Más*
to el norte in the great state of "Wa-ching-ton," you'll find
only sprinklings of Mexicans and that'll beef-up once the
harvest is in. (*Sticks little fruit basket near Washington
state.*)

Following a blast of high political and economic pres-
sure there will be a heavy flow of varied Latinos all over
the central U.S., so many that Chicago... (*Flips over
maps' "Chicago" nameplate to reveal "Chicano."* ...will
change it's name to Chicano, the state of Michigan will
have to change it's name to... (*Flips over "Michigan"
nameplate to reveal "Michoacán."*) ...Michoacán. And the
great state of Utah will have to change it's name because
it sounds too much like *puta*. Ouch!!!

This trend will send Mexicans as far as New York.
Imagine that! (*Singing.*) "Latins in Manhattan," just like
the song. I warn you *not* to call the Puerto Ricans here
"Mexican," they react violently and start dancing ballet in
the streets, just like "West Side Story." It ties up traffic
for hours.

And it's wet in Cuba where Castro has been reigning
for thirty-three years, causing a flood of *gusanos*...
(*Sticks a little troll doll on Florida.*) ...ooops!... I mean
"Cubanos" in South Florida. (*In a Cuban accent.*) ¡Oye,
chico, get an umbrella!

Locally, the air quality will be poor. In fact, with dou-
ble-digit unemployment, earthquakes and floods in California, life everywhere will be real poor...*so* poor you'll
see Latinos moving out of the metropolitan areas into the
central regions, giving the heartland a heart attack.
(*Sticks a Sacred Heart of Jesus on the center of the country.*)

You'll see Columbians in the District of Columbia...
(*Sticks a little 'Yuban' logo on D.C.*) El Salvadoreans
spreading Northward and multiplying like Mexicans.
Dominicans in the Dakotas... (*Sticks a banana on the*

Dakotas.) ...and the Rockies will be wet, with wetbacks. (*Sticks an "Aliens Crossing" highway sign on Rockies.*)

That's the Cultural Climate, good night and have a pleasant *mañana* tomorrow! (*He exits as ...*)

ANNOUNCER: And now, ladies and gentlemen, direct from East Los Angeles, the *chola* in charge...Miss Roseanne Barrio!

Roseanne Barrio

Roseanne Barrio *enters with ratted hair and sweat shirt. She is the gum-chewing, east-side version of "Roseanne." The scene is played as a situation comedy, complete with canned laughter. Center stage are a beat-up sofa and matching coffee table. Our star enters wearing pink fluffy slippers. Vapid music underscores.*

ROSEANNE: (*Calling out the window.*) ...And Chuey, *m'ijo*, you'd better not ditch class again, or you'll be working the left-turn lane on Pico and Alvarado (*Or your local day laborer pick-up area*).

(*She turns around to reveal she is wearing a sweat-shirt reading "Born to Nag."*) Phew! Getting the kids off to school with a healthy breakfast is such a challenge! Thank God for chips and salsa! Time to do my floors. (*From off the table she grabs a spray can, looks down at her slippers and sprays them saying:*) You Spic, you Span. (*She drags her feet to the chair and plops down.*)

Phew! The rewards of being a stay-at-home barrio mom... (*She pops open a beer and turns on the radio.*) ...just me and me and José José alone at last! (*SFX: José José.*)

(*Her daughter, a troubled teen chola, La Twinkles, runs and throws herself on her mother's lap.*) Hey, what are you doing home from school?

TWINKLES: Mommy, Rudy dissed me!

ROSEANNE: That boyfriend of yours. What he do this time? Shoot spit wads at you in homeroom?

TWINKLES: Ick, that's sick. No. He won't give me a baby!

ROSEANNE: (*Shocked.*) A baby?!

TWINKLES: Yeah, and he's still making goo-goo eyes at La Squeaky! What's wrong with me?

ROSEANNE: I raised you right, that's what's wrong with you.

TWINKLES: I'm going off the pill.

ROSEANNE: You'd better mean Flintstone Chewables, *esa*. You're not having a baby.

TWINKLES: But, Mom, I'm just planning ahead. I don't want to have expensive fertility problems like those stressed-out white career women.

ROSEANNE: Believe me, having a baby is the most expensive fertility problem of them all!

TWINKLES: I don't want to be an old mom.

ROSEANNE: Well I don't want to be a young *tata*. Twinkles, *m'ija*, if you had a kid now, I'd be feeding you *both* Mc-Donald's Happy Meals. You'd be fighting over the toy!

TWINKLES: I'm mature enough to make the parental sacrifice and let the baby have my Pocahantas action figure (*Or the latest fast-food merchandising craze.*) …until he falls asleep. And, Mami, a baby means so much. It means I have something of my own. It means I get loved unconditionally. But most important, a baby means I've had an orgasm.

ROSEANNE: No it doesn't. It means *he* had an orgasm. The big "O" is "O"-ver rated.

TWINKLES: (*Disappointed.*) Oh. (*There is a knock at the door. La Twinkles looks out the window.*) It's Rudy! (*She begins primping herself. Rudy enters looking like the "Mother's Worst Fears" poster boy.*)

RUDY: Hi, Mrs. "B."

ROSEANNE: Hi, Rudy, done making license plates for the day? (*He walks over to* La Twinkles *and exchanges a passionate kiss.*)

TWINKLES: (*Dreamily.*) Hi, Rudy. *Ay*, I'm a woman on fire.

ROSEANNE: (*To* Twinkles.) This'll cool ya down. (*She crosses over, spying something on Rudy's neck.*) I see you got a new tattoo. (*Reading.*) To whom it may concern. Love, Rudy. Romantic.

RUDY: I didn't want to do something stupid that I might regret later. If I put a name in there, I'd have it *por vida*. Hey Mrs. B., you got any of that homemade Cup-O-Soup? It was really good!

TWINKLES: Can we make it to go...upstairs?

ROSEANNE: That's it! I'm sending you to that "tough love" Catholic school.

TWINKLES: Our Lady of Perpetual Tuition?

ROSEANNE: No, the all-girl one.

TWINKLES: Not Our Lady of Perpetual Virgins! (La Twinkles *runs off-stage.* Rudy *"coolly" follows.*)

ROSEANNE: Where do you think you're going, you barrio Lothario?

RUDY: To do the job, to dance the horizontal mambo, to be the man!

ROSEANNE: Are you gonna be around when *el* junior's running around in his Huggies, looking for a strong masculine father figure?

RUDY: No, but you are. You're the strongest father figure I know.

ROSEANNE: Well I'm definitely strong. (*She grabs him by the collar.*)

RUDY: Mrs. B., *cuidado*, you're wrinkling my t-shirt. My gang will be dissed. (*Drags him behind the sofa and drops him to the floor, begins punching him.*)

ROSEANNE: How can you let guys with names like "Mousy," "Ringworm" and "Skid-Mark" define who you are,

(*Punch.*) *m'ijo*? You have to have *huevos* (*Knees him. He falls to the floor behind the sofa.*) to stand up to them.

RUDY: (*Pleading.*) They'll take my *huevos* and make machácá! I'm afraid to be free to be me, Mrs. B.

ROSEANNE: Well... (*Smacking him upside the head.*) ...don't be! (*She pulls up a dummy dressed as* Rudy *and proceeds to beat the stuffing out of him.*)

RUDY: (*A disheveled* Rudy *pops up.*) I can't take this double *vida* anymore! (*She gives him a series of "Chinatown" slaps.*) I'm a cholo... (*Slap.*) ...father... (*Slap.*) ...cholo... (*Slap.*) ...father! (*Dazed.*) You're right, Mrs. B. I'll be the faithful father and husband and provider that no one *I know* has ever had. I'll be the perfect husband. (*He passes out and falls behind the sofa.*)

ROSEANNE: (*Stands, straightens herself out, sprays her slippers again, calling out she begins dragging her feet again.*) Oh, La Twinkles, come get your new and improved boyfriend. He's Spic'nSpan...and so's my floor! (*SFX: musical sting canned laughter lights transition to ...*)

Slide: Panza—*big beer belly.*

VOICE OVER: And now for the winners of the best musical group with an eating disorder here are Los Globos, singing "La Panza!"

La Panza

Roadies quickly set up microphones and instruments, then Los Globos, *three hefty cholos, slowly descend onto the stage.*

LOS GLOBOS: (*Singing to the tune of "La Bamba."*)
Para bailar la panza,
Para bailar la panza se necesita una poca de grasa,
Una poca de grasa de comidita
Y harina, y harina

Tortillas de harina comeré
Y chicharrón, soy comelón.

¡Ay, mi panza!
¡Ay, mi panza!
¡Ay, mi panza!
¡Ay, mi panza!

Do you want a *panza*?
If you want a *panza* you've got to eat lots of high carbo
   snack foods,
Lots of high carbo snack foods like gummy bears with a
   side of fudge cake.
Smothered with cookie-dough icecream
That's just the start
It clogs my heart
Here comes a fart.

¡Panza, panza, panza!
¡Panza, panza, panza!
¡Panza, panza, panza!
Chorizo con huevos.

Blackout.

ANNOUNCER: And now, the greatest miracle of the 20th
   Century.

Juan Valdez

VOICES FROM BACKSTAGE: (*In the darkness.*) ¡Juan!
   ¡Juan! ¡Juan! (*Lights up on a Christ-like figure wearing a
   straw hat. It's* Juan Valdez *holding a silver coffee pot in
   his hand.*)
JUAN VALDEZ: I am Juan Valdez. Mine is a simple story of a
   simple, yet humble, yet inconspicuous coffee-bean picker

from the beautiful yet majestic, yet profitable mountains of Colombia. One day a vision came to me. A burning coffee bush spoke to me, whispered in my good ear... "Juan, Juan go forth and spread the word," and the word was Yuban.

Yuban has been good to me, paying me ten cents for every million beans, American money, and they've put my image on every can at every Ralph's. (*He starts to endlessly pick beans.*)

Me and my syphilitic burro Pepe bring you coffee beans that are never picked before their time. Whenever there's a bleary-eyed teamster pulling a double shift, my underpaid sweat is in his thermos. You see, there is a little bit of me in every can at every Ralph's. Wherever there's a trigger-happy punchy postal worker, some pus from my one good eye is in his coffee-stained "Have A Nice Day" mug. Wherever there's a governor vetoing César Chávez Day, there's residual pesticides coating the bottom of his Limoge demitasse.

Me and my beans are with you along with my disciples: Capuccino, Café Mocha, Café Latte. My beans are everywhere. Drink my blood, my pain, my sweat...drink Yuban. Good to the last drop. (*He falls in the floor from exhaustion.*)

ANNOUNCER: This message brought to you by Yuban, the proud sponsor of the LA LA Awards.

(Lights transition to ...)

And now Spain's best export since Christopher Columbus, more Suave than Bolla, the star of Melanie Griffith's personal home videos ... Mr. Antonio Nalgueras.

Antonio Nalgueras

With his sexy black hair pulled back in a ponytail, Antonio Nalgueras *enters. He wears a padded derriere and dances*

backwards, ravishing rump proudly displayed toward the
audience. He stops center stage and spins around.

ANTONIO: Good evening, *mambo*! I'm Antonio Nalgueras,
and I'm not too sexy for my jeans, *mambo*! You're probably wondering how I became so sexy. No, it's not the two
pounds of Brylcream in my hair, or the quarter pounder
in my pants. It just comes naturally.

   I can't help it, I never could. You know, even as a
child I was very sexy. My mother used to love to change
my diapers just to look at my buns. *Mambo*! But I must
confess to you, my adoring fans, and I've tried to adore as
many of you as I possibly could, and you know who you
are. *Mambo*!

   I must confess how tough it is to be a Latin sex sym-
bol. *Ay*, the performance anxiety. So many duties to per-
form. *Mambo*!

   I must speak fluent body language, the language of
love. *Ethpañol. Te quiero tanto, querida, pero tengo ham-*
bre, y deseo una paella o arroz con pollo. Mambo! Sounds
good, doesn't it? I said, "I love you so much, but I'm hun-
gry and I want some *paella* or chicken and rice." Works
every time.

   Almodóvar discovered me in BarTHelona, where sexy
people like me are born. I was a waiter at a topless *tapas*
bar, slinging sangría for disgusting tourists from Ger-
many. They're so unsexy. They sound like there is something stuck in their throats when they speak.
Farfegnugen. ¡Ay, Dios mío! How can you seduce anyone
with that language? *Mambo*!

   Oh, before I forget, please catch my next film where I
act with only my hair and, *por supuesto*, that's *Ethpañol*,
my buns. A tour de force. *Mambo*!

   The next category is "Best actress in a movie starring
a bleeding-heart liberal who wants to act in a mainstream
minority project." The nominees are María María as the

Maid María and Meryl Estripada as Mrs. Wright in their riveting performance in "Cry Me Over the Border." Let's take a look at a live re-enactment clip.

"Cry Me Over the Border"

Faint indigenous music underscores as Meryl Estripada *as* Mrs. Wright *enters. She is attired in designer jogging togs and faces off with* María María *as* María, *a young urban Latina.*

MARÍA: (*No accent.*) I really need this job, Mrs. Wright.

MRS. WRIGHT: I know you're nervous. This maid, er... housekeeper job is an opportunity for you to lift yourself out of the pain of the barrio.

MARÍA: "The pain of the barrio?..."

MRS. WRIGHT: María, don't worry about being a stereotype, there's a lot of truth in them. Tell me about your poverty, about the terror that made you run across five lanes of freeway to get to this country. Tell me about your pain...

MARÍA: (Not getting it) Pain?...

MRS. WRIGHT: María, I am trying to like you. I'm on the board of UNICEF. We deal with Third-World people like you all the time...—

MARÍA: But I'm not a Third-World type...

MRS. WRIGHT:— ...Intrinsically oppressed indigenous brown people. Tell me about the curse of your childhood...just tell me the truth, god damnit.

MARÍA: Well, actually, I had a pretty nice childhood...

MRS. WRIGHT: Honey, I don't think I can use you. For fifty cents a day, I have adopted more children than Sally Struthers. I know how rickety they can get...you seem too...robust.

MARÍA: I had infectious hepatitis when I was one-and-a-half years old.

MRS. WRIGHT: That's so sad...good!

MARÍA: I had twelve, no... (*Starts putting on a thick Mexican accent.*) ...twenty brothers and *seesters*.

MRS. WRIGHT: Twenty-one kids! How many died?

MARÍA: They all died...real slow. Except for my brother Tico, who had to live in an iron lung. Off and on...uh...whenever we had electricity.

MRS. WRIGHT: You're the real thing! Give me more!

MARÍA: (*Thinking hard.*) I lived in a small village, one horse, one toilet, one volcano. It erupted twice a day. Lava would burn our feet. It hurts even now. Ouch! (*She starts fanning her feet then coughs.*)

MRS. WRIGHT: What's that?

MARÍA: My lungs, they're shot because I breathed ash all the time.

MRS. WRIGHT: I hope that doesn't mean you can't work seven days a week!

MARÍA: Oh, no!

MRS. WRIGHT: That's what I like about you people. You have such a work ethic.

MARÍA: (*In the spirit.*) We lived with two cows, four *cheeckens* and a partridge in a pear tree. And we were the lucky ones.... We had a corrugated cardboard roof over our heads. And then there were gangs, with their machete drive-bys in their lowriders...

MRS. WRIGHT: Lowriders?

MARÍA: Uh, their *burros*...little midget *burros*.

MRS. WRIGHT: Midget *burros*?

MARÍA: Midget, lowrider *burros*.

MRS. WRIGHT: Oh, María!

MARÍA: ¡Ay, Mrs. Wright! I was kidnapped and dragged through the jungles of Club Med when I was twelve. He was much older—thirteen.

MRS. WRIGHT: You poor *neena*! Did you report it to the police?

MARÍA: He _was_ the police! The Chief of Police. He said I
   shouldn't be out in the jungle at that time of night.

MRS. WRIGHT: Gloria Allred says that it is a woman's right
   to be in the jungle at any damn time she pleases. Did he
   throw you down?

MARÍA: Yes.

MRS. WRIGHT: Was he cute?

MARÍA: Yes.

MRS. WRIGHT: Did he look like Andy García?

MARÍA: Yes.

MRS. WRIGHT: (*Gushing.*) Yummy!

MARÍA: I struggled. He kissed me...

MRS. WRIGHT: How did he kiss you?

MARÍA: Real deep. And there our Aztec love lust was consum-
   mated to the pounding rhythms of the ocean on the sandy
   shores of Cozumel... and this is Andy García, mind you...
   There, I finally succumbed to his overwhelming passion,
   and in that evil union I relived the conquest of the cosmic
   race of Aztlán! ¡*Qué viva México*!

MRS. WRIGHT: ¡*Qué viva México*! You're hired! I'm going to
   feel so much better about myself. (*They both exit laughing,* Antonio Nalgueras *returns.*)

ANTONIO: ...And the winner is María María. Mamboriffic
   performance! (María María, *still in braids, runs to the
   podium.* Antonio *hands her an award.*)

MARÍA: (*Now with an excitable Hollywood starlet attitude.*) I
   can't believe that I won for best actress. I've never won
   anything in my life. Are you sure the judges didn't make a
   mistake? I'll give it back. I just want to thank my braids,
   who made it all happen. You like them! You like them!
   You really like my braids! (*She exits.*)

Best Latino Film

ANTONIO: She's a truly mambolicious performer. We now reach the pinnacle, or what I call the *"Mambo* Moment," the LA LA Award for Best Latino Film.

Since so few Latino films are made each year, we've included the last ten years of films into the category. So the nominees are: "Alive!," a true story about a South American soccer team that went on a crash diet. "The Mambo Queens," *my* movie about two Cuban transvestites struggling to make it in New York. The pay was lousy, but I got to keep my ponytail. The angry sequel to "Schindler's List," called "Schindler's Shit List"... Do you realize he didn't save one Mexican from being killed by the Nazis? "Like Water for CocoPuffs"...a cookbook made into a movie and the biggest grossing Mexican film since "Cantinflas Versus Don Francisco." A gay version of "El Mariachi" called "El Liberachi"... I saw this piece of *mierda* and the leading man's performance was tripe compared to my sensitive portrayal of a gay Latino in my film, "Philadelphia Cream Cheese"...available in your supermarket's dairy case under the heading "sour queen"...*mambo*! "My Dysfunctional Familia," a story of a proud, loving, stable Mexican-American family...for us that *is* dysfunctional. And the final nominee, "My *Chola Loca*," a tragic mix of gunplay and hair spray. (*SFX: Fanfare. Slide: Cast and director of "My* Vida Loca.*")*

And the winner is, of course, a film which was written and directed by a Caucasian, "The Making of My *Chola Loca*," which apparently was more violent than the actual film itself. Let's look at a live re-enactment clip right now!

"The Making of 'My *Chola Loca*'"

Barry, *a nerdy director, tries to assemble his slow-moving cast and crew.*

BARRY: Break's over. I'm the director, and we are going over budget. Let's get back to work. (*Two actresses enter:* Sad Girl, *a hard-as-nails chola, and* Wendy, *a busty Jewish-American vixen trying to break into show "biz" by playing a chola with big hair.* Barry *starts the action by placing the girls face to face in switchblade combat.*) "My *Chola Loca*," scene one, take twenty-two. Marker. (*Slaps clap board shut.*) Speed. Rolling. Action!

SAD GIRL: (*In a heavy chola accent*) ...And if you ever throw *el mal ojo* at me or any of my home girls again, I'm gonna cut your pretty face up like *machacá*!

WENDY: (*In a heavy Bronx accent.*) Yeah, I'm gonna kick your ass and all your *homos*!

SAD GIRL: Oh shit! (Barry *runs onto set screaming, helps* Wendy *up and pulls her aside.*)

BARRY: "Homos?" Cut! Wendy, the word's "homies"..."homos" is an entirely different type of gang.

WENDY: Sorry, Mr. Jones.

BARRY: That's "HONAYS," Wendy. In Spanish the j's sound like h's.

WENDY: Sorry, Mr. Hones.

BARRY: (*To* Wendy.) Later... (*To* Sad Girl.) Okay, *carnala*, we're gonna go for another take! (*All moan.*)

SAD GIRL: Oh man, this is really *stoopid*, she's only gonna mess it up again! Why did you hire her anyways?

BARRY: Because I couldn't find a real *chola* with acting experience.

SAD GIRL: Bullshit! I've done 'em all! "Colors," "Boulevard Nights," "Ghetto Blaster," "Independence Day."

WENDY: There were no Chicanas in "Independence Day."

SAD GIRL: Screw you, I ended up on the cutting-room floor. Me and *the aliens* were like this (*She crosses fingers.*) ...everyone kept confusing us.

BARRY: Discuss the summer blockbusters later.

BARRY: (*Shouting.*) Hey, where's Faye? Faye! Faye! (*Wearing a huge* chola *wig and clad in a tube-top and tight skirt which exposes a hairy midriff,* Fea, *the ugliest girl in the hood, saunters onto the set. She is applying lipstick.* Fea *is usually played by a hairy man in drag.*)

FEA: Hey, Mr. Gabacho director, the name is "Fea." It means "ugly."

BARRY: Okay, Fea, we're going to do the cat-fight scene, "My *Chola Loca*," And action!

BARRY: (*Slaps clap board shut.*) Speed. Rolling. Action!

SAD GIRL: You think you're a tough *chavala*, eh? I was gang banging when you were just finger-spray painting

FEA: My homegirls voted me *ruca* most likely to have a crack baby!

SAD GIRL: That's nothing, I *am* a crack baby!

WENDY: That's nothing. My old man is so tough that he's got a bull's eye tattooed on his chest.

SAD GIRL: Ha! That's nothing My old man survived so many drive-bys, his Nickname's Swiss Cheese. (*The girls face-off.*)

WENDY: I'll rip your tube-top...

FEA: ...I'll break your eyeliner.

SAD GIRL: ...I'll smash your hairdo.

WENDY: (TO FEA) ...I'll shave your legs!

BARRY: (*Running back in.*) Cut! That was awful. What we're striving for here is *realism*!

SAD GIRL: (*Challenging him.*) What do you know about being Latino?

BARRY: Everything! I adore *menudo* and I drive a Cordoba.

FEA: (*Closing in on him.*) Wow. Rich Corinthian Leather!

BARRY: (*Nervously.*) I've always been fascinated by you people. Fea, did you know that you wear a lot of eyeliner because the Aztecs used to worship the raccoon?

FEA: Am I wearing too much eyeliner?

BARRY: Oh, no!! The camera loves it! And you, Sad Girl, your ratted-up hair signifies your reaching for the ancient Aztec God Quetzalcoatl.

SAD GIRL: Fuck you, man!

WENDY: Barry, when are we gonna do the lesbian nude scene?

FEA: Lesbian nude scene?

SAD GIRL: No way, *buey*!

BARRY: Way, it's a rewrite! The ancient Aztec civilization practiced human sacrifice, and sometimes the sacrificial virgins would turn to each other and comfort and caress each other in the nude.

SAD GIRL: Well in the ancient Mayan civilization the sacrificial girls wore pasties.

WENDY: I'll do it!

SAD GIRL: I won't.

FEA: (*Drops his tube-top to expose his flat hairy nipples.*) I will.

ALL: (*Recoiling.*) Yuck! Fea!

BARRY: We'll use a body double.

FEA: You've hurt my feelings. (*Exits crying.*)

BARRY: Come on, girls, do this for your people, for your *gente*, for your *raza*! (*SFX: Sounds of screeching tires and approaching gunfire.*)

WENDY: ...What's that?

SAD GIRL: It's a drive-by, run! (Sad Girl *expertly ducks the bullets and runs off-stage.*)

WENDY: (*Exits screaming.*) Barry, duck, you'll get shot!

BARRY: My movie's gonna have a real drive-by! Boy, oh boy! (*He gets shot, clutches his chest and falls to the ground, happily exclaiming:*) I think we've got a hit!

The Coup

ANNOUNCER: And the winner of the media image award is the multi-talented Juan José Valentino "the Gang-Banger" Jiménez. (Juan José Valentino "The Gang-Banger" Jiménez *enters wearing an absurd compilation costume: big greaser wig, headband, serape, bandoleers and sombrero. He clutches a knife in one hand and an award in the other. He enters joyfully screaming.*)

JUAN JOSÉ VALENTINO: (*Thick Pepino from "The Real McCoys"-type accent.*) My name is José Valentino "The Killer" Jiménez. ¡Ajúa! I won! I won! ¡Gané! Gracias, thank-joo, *gracias*. I'm berry honored to asept thees aguard. I like tu tank all da peoples who made me possible, all the tv, radio, newspapers, da writers, directors and costume designers who didn't do their research.

   And now, I would like to do a medley of my hits. (*A la bandito.*) Ay, ay, ay. ¡Arriba, arriba, andale, andale! (*A la gang member.*) I'm gonna cut up your pretty face like *machacá*! (*A la Latin lover.*) Mambo! I'm not too sexy for my serape! I won! I won!

   I will forever be the Latino's image! I won! (*One blood-curdling scream from* Diane *in the house.* José Valentino "The Gang-Banger" Jiménez *freezes and house lights go up.*)

DIANE: Stop! Please this can't go on. Excuse me. Look at that up there, it's a stereotype-mutant; it's just the thing we're trying to get rid of. (Diane, Armando *and* Luisa *enter and surround* Juan José. *Realizing that he is outnumbered, he exits running. More protesters enter carrying signs and chanting.*)

ALL: The media's portrayal.

Has been one big betrayal.

ARMANDO: (*Stopping audience.*) Don't panic, ladies and gents. Everything's under control. I'm from the Latins Anonymous Liberation Front. And what we're going to do to you is going to be painful... I mean painless. We are going to take back control of our image. I'm Armando Molina (*The actor's real name.*), I'm a Colombian immigrant (*The actor's real nationality.*) ...and I've never done cocaine or been in in a welfare office. Okay, I've never done cocaine *in* a welfare office. (The Protesters *jump on stage.*)

LUISA: Hi, I'm Luisa (*The actor's real name and an ironic statement of mistaken racism.*) and I'm the proud mother of a blond-haired, blue-eyed boy. I'm his real mom, yet, when I take him to the park, people ask me if I'm his maid. I sort of am, but that's beside the point.

DIANE: Ladies and gentlemen, I'm Diane Rodriguez... (*Another actor introduces herself using her real name and background.*) ...I am a Chicana and this is what I look like. Well, I look a little better in the morning. I'm a little tired right now. (*Excited,* Cris *enters carrying a guitar.*)

CRIS: Everything's under control. Our tape is cued up in the sound booth. Biff, the stage manager, is tied up and Cuco is in control.

DIANE: (*Calming* Cris *down.*) Cris, honey, we've already taken over the show. Introduce yourself.

CRIS: Hi, my name is Cris, I'm a Mexican national. (HE HOLDS UP HIS WALLET AND PULLS OUT CARDS.) This is my green card, here's my gold card and here's my Alamo Rent-A-Car Card.

DIANE: Cris, Luisa, Armando and I are regular people...no headbands, no accents, no media coverage. The media ignores us 'cause we don't make good copy. We are this country's *desaparecidos*. But we refuse to remain silent.

ARMANDO: Yeah, we risked our lives trying to reach you. While we were outside trying to get in, we were almost killed out there on Hollywood Boulevard (*Or street your theatre is on.*).

DIANE: Some lady in a pink Pinto almost ran me over.

ARMANDO: And after the fourth time we were thrown out of the theatre, dodging on-coming cars at ninety-five miles per hour, we wrote a little song about the latest victims of stereotyping. If this song is a hit, we're going to call our group Las Mamás y Las Puras Papás.

DIANE: Does everyone have their lyrics? (*They all take out their lyrics, which are written on a crumpled paper bag and styrofoam cup.* Armando *has it written on his hand.*)

CRIS: Does everyone have their keys? (*All hit a very sour note.*) Ready or not, hit the tape.

ARMANDO: The following song is dedicated to all of you: the immigrants.

The Mamás and the Papás

The men sing the following to the tune of "California Dreamin'." Everything italicized is sung by the women.

All our faces are brown... *And America's scared.*
So the borders are closed... *Pete Wilson's a pendejo.*

I've been for a walk... *Across five lanes of freeway.*
To find a job today... *One you wouldn't take, anyway.*

I'd be safe and warm... *paying Uncle Sam my taxes.*
If I was in L.A.... *Making minimum wage at Denny's.*
California Dreamin'... *California dreamin'.*
There's 20,000,000 on their way!

Communism's dead... *We're the scapegoats now!*
Lockheed's gone the same way... *Lost your job today.*

Your home was worth four-hundred thousand dollars.
Now you can't give it away... *Go refinance today.*

So you blame it on the Mexicans... *other immigrants too.*
Pete Wilson's having a field day... *it's the American way.*

California Dreamin',
Your grandpa got here the same way.

(Musical break.)

DIANE: *(Spoken.)*
Do aliens have inalienable rights? We think so.

LUISA: *(Spoken.)*
Imagine an America with no immigrants. Imagine no
sushi bars, no baklava, no shwarme or derma.

CRIS: You all look beautiful tonight. As I look at you, I'm sure
that if I shook any of your family trees, an immigrant...
perhaps an illegal one... would fall out.

ARMANDO:
Imagine an America with no immigrants and you can
imagine all of you gone.

ALL: *(Singing resumes.)*
But I'm taking classes... *At Junior College L.A.*
Get an MBA... *My computer's on its way.*
Then we'll kick some asses... *Take the good jobs away.*
Isn't that the paranoia in L.A....

It's really stupid complaining about immigrants.
America was built this *pinche* way.

California Dreamin'... Your grandpa got here the same
way.
California Dreamin'... Relax and learn to say "José."
California Dreamin'... Your grandpa got here the same
way!

The Cosmic Race

Lights fade on the quartet, silhouetting them as slides of immigrants arriving at various times in history, the Statue of Liberty, Ross Perot, Chinese internment camps, grape pickets, César Chávez and Ellis Island are framed against images of Hollywood stereotypes, such as Zorro, Latin Spitfire, banditos, etc....

The music and visuals accelerate and end with a loud alarm clock going off. The sound fades to the quiet strings of a "weeping guitar."

One of the final two slides is a quote from César Chávez: "And in the end we will win." A quote from José Vasconselos, Mexican philosopher, follows: "The red, white, yellow, black... America is home to all of them. In America we are creating a new race, la raza cósmica, *the cosmic race."*

Lights out.

Fin

Notes on Expanding the Show

Although the "LA LA Awards" was originally written to be performed by its four creators, Cris Franco, Luisa Leschin, Armando Molina, Diane Rodriguez, it lends itself well to being expanded. Local drama students can participate as protesters at the start and end of the show. Glamorous male and female starlets can escort the star presenters to and from the podium. Mary Qué makes a splash if she enters with two boys on a leash. Juan Valdez can be preaching to a flock of on-stage followers, all clutching cups of coffee, which he refills throughout his sermon. The crew of "My *Chola Loca*" consists of script girls, sound-boom operators, cameramen, etc.... Finally, an intermission break can be added between "The Cultural Climate" and "Roseanne Barrio" by having protester's stop the show after Maclovio is done with his weather report and they chase him off-stage. The management then calls for an intermission to bring things back to order.

Latins Anonymous

by

Luisa Leschin
Armando Molina
Rick Nájera
Diane Rodríguez

LATINS ANONYMOUS premiered at the Los Angeles Theater Center on September 15, 1989 and ran until March 4, 1989 with the following original cast: Luisa Leschin, Armando Molina, Rick Najera, and Diane Rodriguez.

Jose Cruz Gonzales / Miguel Delgado	Co-Directors
Jose Lopez	Lighting Design
Patssi Valdez	Costumes
Miguel Delgado	Choreography
Gabriella Fernández	Accesories/Props
Nathan Stein	Sound Design
Ken Short	Set Design
Tony Villareal	Hat Design

Act I

Scene:	Written by:
Meeting 1*	Group
Samuel Espada	Leschin
Meeting 2-Amends	Group
Joaquín in Love	Molina
Menudo	Nájera
Meeting 3	Group
Latch Key Kids	Nájera
Meeting 4	Group
Separate Turf	Nájera

Act II

Scene:	Written by:
Meeting 5	Group
Hermana Petra	Rodríguez
Machos of Omaha	Nájera
Lolana Aerobics	Leschin
Armando Trained	Molina/Lisa Loomer
Calvino de Kline	Leschin
Mexican-American	Nájera
Las Comadres	Leschin
Pinataphobia Therapy	Group
Mayan Defense League	Rodríguez
Meeting 6	Group

*"Shares" are written by the individual performers.

The Characters

NICOLETTE/LUISA: Late 20's-mid 30's. Suffers from Latin Denial.

The actress playing NICOLETTE/LUISA also plays BLOND FEMME FATAL in *Samuel Espada*, BITSY in *Park Bench*, MARÍA in *Latch Key Kids*, Puerto Rican MARÍA in *Separate Turf*, LOLANA in *Lolana Aerobics*, LUPE in *Las Comadres* and LUCY GARCE in *The Mayan Defense League*.

DIANE: Mid 30's-late 30's. A hard core Chicana who's now asking "What about me?"

The actress playing DIANE also plays the MOTHER in *Latch Key Kids*, MEXICAN MARÍA in *Separate Turf*, HERMANA PETRA in *Hermana Petra*, VANITA in *Machos of Omaha*, DOLORES in *Las Comadres* and OBSIDIAN BUTTERFLY in *The Mayan Defense League*.

RICK: Late 20's-mid 30's. A Mexican-American living on the hyphen.

The actor playing RICK also plays SAMUEL ESPADA in *Samuel Espada*, TEEN IDOL in *Menudo*, JUAN in *Latch Key Kids*, MEXICAN CHANO in *Separate Turf*, JUAN in *Machos of Omaha* and SNAKE BREATH in *The Mayan Defense League*.

ARMANDO: Mid 30's-late 30's. A sensitive kind of guy trapped in a macho kind of body.

The actor playing ARMANDO also plays JOAQUÍN in *Park Bench*, RESTAURANT MANAGER in *Menudo*, the FATHER in *Latch Key Kids*, CHINO in *Separate Turf*, the ANNOUNCER in *Hermana Petra*, FIDEL in *Machos of Omaha*, PEPE in *Las Comadres* and JAGUAR in *The Mayan Defense League*.

The Set

Like the actors, the set must be versatile enough to take us from a meeting hall to a park bench to a restaurant quickly. These effects are best created with lighting, sound effects and minimal props. Some of the designs have attempted to meld Aztec imagery with contemporary urban imagery in an effort to capture the full range of stories that are told.

The Style

The panorama of theatrical styles presented in Latins Anonymous *goes from realistic (the Latins Anonymous meetings and shares) to broad sketch-comedy (*Separate Turf*) to* Teatro Chicano-meets-Sci-Fi *(*Mayan Defense League*). Costumes support these styles by having the ensemble dressed in basic black for all the meeting and shares, and bold, colorful wardrobe worn for all the other sketches.*

Act One

In darkness we hear a radio surfing from station to station. Within the static we hear generic news, music in both English and Spanish, interspersed with the following:

RADIO ANNOUNCER V.O.: Stay tuned for the Hermana Petra Show with her tambourine and her army of sisters, alleluia. Brought to you by Dos Equis. (*Radio FX.*)

RADIO ANNOUNCER V.O.: The Menudo concert will be brought to you by Calvino de Kline, fine Fragrances. "Oh, the smell of it!" (*Radio surfing continues as lights fade up on four people in silhouette. The radio segues into a commercial for "Latins Anonymous." Pachelbel Canon in "D" softly plays underneath.*)

RADIO ANNOUNCER V.O.: It's three A.M. and you're staring bleary-eyed into a bowl of matzo ball soup. Your girlfriend

Buffy hands you a corned beef on rye. You're trying to forget that your name is Hernández. You've got a problem. Try Latins Anonymous. Only a phone call away. (*Lights to half revealing the four actors frozen in silhouette. Lights up.*)

Meeting 1

*A Latins Anonymous meeting. *The name of the local town where the production is taking place should be used every time a local reference is made.*

DIANE: Welcome to Latins Anonymous. Why don't we get the meeting started!

RICK: Hi, my name is Rick.

ALL: (*Encouraging the audience to join in.*) Hi, Rick.

RICK: And I admit I'm a Latino.

DIANE: Hi, my name is Diane.

ALL: Hi, Diane.

DIANE: And I admit I'm a Latina.

ARMANDO: Hi, my name is Armando.

ALL: Hi, Armando.

ARMANDO: And I admit I'm a Latino.

DIANE: I'd like to welcome our newest member, Nicolette. Let's support her. Let's give her a big hand! (*She encourages everyone to applaud.*)

NICOLETTE: (*With a thick French accent.*) Merci beaucoup. I am not a new memburr. I am viziting, strictly viziting forr tonight onlay.

DIANE: Well, welcome anyway, Nicolette. Now, before we go on, I just have to say that I feel very honored to have been asked to lead this "Hollywood* (**Local city's name*)" meeting, and, boy, do I need a meeting. (*They all take a needy drag of their cigarettes.*) Now, ours is a three-step program and I'd like to ask Rick if he would read the "Traditions." (*Hands him the Latins Anonymous book.*)

RICK: Hi, my name is Rick.

ALL: Hi, Rick.

RICK: (*Reading.*) We admit we are Latin, powerless to change
   that, and don't want to.

DIANE AND ARMANDO: Absolutely. Yes!

RICK: We are not afraid to take a long look at ourselves and
   realize that we don't have to boycott every single major
   food group there is. We admit we have been silent for too
   long, and strive to awaken from the imperialistic oppres-
   sion of our colonial past, and seek to end the colonization
   of our minds by the oppressive Conquistadors (Rick *loses*
   control.) ...and those little white kids at school who used
   to call me "wetback, wetback, wetback."

DIANE: Rick, are you okay?

RICK: I get so emotional sometimes. I guess it's my Latino
   nature. We're a passionate people.

DIANE: Thank you, Rick. Thank you for sharing that with us.
   Armando, the four H's. (Rick *and* Diane *come downstage*
   to join him. Nicolette *tries to sneak out.*)

DIANE: Nicolette?

NICOLETTE: (*Busted.*) Oui, Oui. (*She joins the group.*)

ARMANDO: Yes, the four H's to live by:
   We're not Hispanic
   We're not Humble
   We're not Hostile
   We don't Hassle anyone about it. Damn it!

RICK: As treasurer of the (**Hollywood.*) Chapter of Latins
   Anonymous, I'd like to say that I invested your dues
   money in some excellent high-yield junk bonds.

DIANE: Thank you, I think, Rick. Let's begin our shares, but
   try to keep them short. If you get stuck, I'll read off this
   list of possible topics. (*Reading.*) "Latin Denial," (*They*
   look accusingly at Nicolette.) "Latin Flirtation: how to grip
   it..." I mean, "...how to get a grip on it." "Piñata Phobia,"
   "Machismo in America," "Sex with Anglos"...

ARMANDO: Me, me, me!!!

RICK: No, me!

DIANE: (*Rips list, gives each one half.*) Okay, share an Anglo. Now, we usually give our newcomers a chance to share first, and there are a lot of newcomers here tonight so... I'm going to ask you (*Selecting someone from the audience.*) ...to just stand up and tell us something about yourself. (*Encouraging audience member to share their name, where they live, etc., then sees* Nicolette.) Oh, I'm sorry Nicolette should really share first. She's our newest member. (*To audience member.*) Sit down. Nicolette, why don't you tell us a little about yourself, please.

NICOLETTE: Certainment. Bonsoir, my name 'eez Neekolette.

ALL: *Bonsoir*, Nicolette. (*All three sitting.*)

NICOLETTE: And, I admeet to absolutely nozing. I am only 'ere to support mon ami, Armando een 'eez effort to deal wiz 'eez identity crisis. 'e 'az told me you are a group of Spanish people wiz a lot of problems due to your ettnicitay. I can only zank God I know 'oo and what I am so clearly, Dieu merci. I 'ave a leetel somezing in common wiz you. My fazer was Spanish, but from Spain... BarTHelona... But, eet really 'ad no effect on me whatzoever. Een fact, I am so un-Latin zat I am sure I was adopted. As you can tell, I am Française (pronounced Françez). My mozer 'eez Française, so bien sûr, I am Française. I love being Française. I was born in Paree, went to school in Monte Carlo, went to finishing school in Geneve, that 'eez La Suisse...

DIANE: (*Cutting her off with bell.*) Excuse me, Nicolette. We like to keep it short.

NICOLETTE: I 'ope you all get better very soon. *Merci.*

DIANE: Good share.

RICK: I'd like to share.

DIANE: Certainly.

RICK: Hi, my name is Rick...

ALL: Hi, Rick.

RICK: And I admit I am Latino—Mexican-American to be
  exact. I first found out I was Latino when I was nine
  years old. I told my mom I wanted to play with the Mexican kids down the street, and she said you *are* Mexican,
  so you can stay home and play with yourself. But I got
  bored with that and I was afraid of going blind. So, I went
  to the schoolyard and played with the American kids
  because I'm Mexican-*American*. But an Anglo kid there
  called me a wetback. It didn't sound like a bad name...
  wetback, dryback, quarterback, halfback, wetback. I did-
  n't know if he'd insulted me or not, so to play it safe I
  punched him out. I got sent back to the school supervisor.
  He said, (*Imitating him.*) "Why'd you strike Bradley?"
  "Because he called me a wetback." "Well, are you Mexican?" he asked. "Yes," I said. "Well, then you are a wetback." I just want to say that for the first time in my life,
  thanks to all of you, I feel like I have a home. Thank you
  for my one-year tortilla chip!
DIANE: Congratulations, Rick. Congratulations. Yes. Yes.
  And as we say...
DIANE, ARMANDO AND RICK: Keep coming back. It
  works!!!

Blackout. In the darkness a saxophone wails 40's style.

Samuel Espada, P.P.I.

Under the plaintive sounds of a wailing sax, Samuel
Espada *enters with trenchcoat and fedora, stops under a street-
light, reflectively lights a cigarette, as the lights rise.*

ESPADA: It's five A.M. in the A.M. and here I am, walking
  down these mean streets getting ready to experience
  another tequila sunrise. My eyes feel like two prickly
  cacti. I'd give my left...whatever...to be home catching
  some zees next to my faithful girlfriend Conchita. But no.
  I'm on a case. Me, Samuel Espada, P.P.I.—Private Pachu-

co Investigator. I'm facing one of the toughest cases of my career.

I had been hired by the entire Latin female population of this God-forsaken Tex-Mex town to find out one thing: why Latin men have this compulsion...this drive...this need...to date blonde women. (*A Blonde Femme Fatale, whose face we never see slinks across the stage and leans provocatively against a lamppost.*)

Dames, dames, damn those dames. Dames are a mystery no one can solve. Except me...Samuel Espada, P.P.I. Hello, Blondie! (*As Samuel sees her he lets out a Mexican grito.*) Sorry, I'm on the job. (*He slowly circles her.*)

I know you. I know your kind. What's your name? Wendy? Debbie? Susie? Buffie? Binky? (*He takes her in his arms.*) The name says it all...long gams, blue peepers...white girls! What is it about you Aryan cheerleaders that makes us Latin men feel like piñatas when we date you? What? What? What? (*They begin a seductive Apache dance.*)

First you cling to me like cheap perfume just because I'm Latino. Yeah, Latino makes me a macho. Latino makes me a good lover. Hey, that's no lie. Sure, I'm a good dick. (*She reaches for his groin.*) Get your mind out of the gutter! It means detective. I know what the turn-ons are about you ash-blonde babes. You buy all my lines...not even my good stuff. (*The Blonde is wrapped around him, fondling a scar on his cheek.*)

What's this you ask? Oh, I got this scar in a bullfight. Ha! All I have to do is talk Spanish to her and it's all over." Wendy, my *amor...mi corazón*! *¿Dónde esta la biblioteca?*" (*She faints into his arms.*) This is a definite turn-on! But the next minute you give me the cold shoulder! (*She kicks him across the stage and pins his hand to the ground with her stiletto heel.*) You give me the deep freeze, the Arctic chill. You tell your friends I'm your gardener when you see me at the mall. You make me feel so low I could be sitting on a dime and my feet wouldn't touch the ground. Why am I so attracted to you, Blondie? Don't make me bark like a dog! Arf, arf! I hate that! (*Crawls after her, succumbing.*)

Look at you. Maybe it's because you remind me of wheat fields, of apple pie, of little Kim O'Flannery from my fourth-grade class who was so blonde she glowed. You remind me of the American Dream. A dream I am not a part of. Ouch...that cut through me like the bullet I bit in Iwo Jima. (*Disentangling himself and pushing her away.*)

Ha! You almost got me, you blonde, black widow spider. But no! I'm going home to wrap myself around Conchita... Conchita! She's brown as the holster on my .32 snubnose, eyes so dark you can show a movie in them. When I look into her eyes I see...ME. My family...my home... My American Dream. ¡Orale!

Lights slowly fade out as Espada *strikes a pachuco pose.*

Amends

VOICE OVER: THE THIRD STEP: MAKE AMENDS TO THOSE YOU HAVE HURT. (*The four Anonymous members are staggered about the stage. The scene is played in black. Each actor holds a flashlight which he flashes in his face each time he speaks, then turns off.*)

RICK: I'd like to make amends for the Alamo. Sorry we won. (*Bell chimes.*)

DIANE: I'd like to make amends to my throat for all the *gritos* I've thrown. *Ay ay ay ay ay.* (*Coughs.*)

ARMANDO: (*Bell chimes.*) I'd like to make amends to my grandmother for all the times I yelled, "Speak English!"

NICOLETTE: (*Bell chimes.*) Um, ah...

RICK: (*Bell chimes.*) I'd like to make amends to all my Spanish teachers. *Yo me* sorry...

DIANE: (*Bell chimes.*) I'd like to make amends for trading my (*Fernando Valenzuela) baseball card for a (*_____). (*Current "Anglo" star baseball player.*)

ARMANDO: (*Bell chimes.*) I'd like to make amends to all the fruit vendors on the Hollywood Freeway. I prefer to shop at Lucky's.

NICOLETTE: (*Bell chimes. Light on, says nothing, light off.*)

RICK: (*Bell chimes.*) I'd like to make amends to my chihuahua Pepe for putting him up against Chuck's Doberman. Sorry, Pepe.

DIANE: (*Bell chimes.*) I'd like to make amends to my nephew for insisting he be called Xochipile Cuhautémoc.

ARMANDO: (*Bell chimes.*) I'd like to make amends to all the women I told I was related to Julio Iglesias. (*Bell chimes. They all turn to* Nicolette.*)

NICOLETTE: I would like to make amendz for absolutely nozing.

Bell chimes. All flashlights off. Blackout.

Joaquín in Love—A Nuyorican Seduction

A bench near Washington Square Park, New York. It's late afternoon. We hear romantic strains of Rodrigo's "Concierto de Aranjuez." Joaquín, a Puerto Rican poet, sits reading a well-worn copy of the poems of Rimbaud. Bitsy, a young, nerdy N.Y.U. student, enters, watches the pigeons, sits on the bench.

JOAQUÍN: (*Discovering her.*) Who created you? Rimbaud created you! You read Rimbaud?

BITSY: Yes.

JOAQUÍN: So do I. This poem, it's for you.

BITSY: For me?

JOAQUÍN: (*Reading.*) "A Season in Hell," by Arthur Rimbaud. "I swallowed a terrific mouthful of poison, my entrails are burning. I am dying of thirst. I can't cry out. The air of

Hell does not permit hymns. I think I am in Hell, there-
fore, I am." (*With a flourish.*) Ahh!

BITSY: That was beautiful.

JOAQUÍN: Now you read Rimbaud to me.

BITSY: (*Reading.*) "Like a God with large blue eyes... (*Notic-
ing his eyes are brown.*) brown eyes and a snow body, the
sea and the sky entice to the marble stairs the swarm of
young, strong roses on the rosebush." I don't know what
that means.

JOAQUÍN: What Rimbaud is trying to say is the thorns on
the rosebush, ripping your leg from the limb, the blood
splashing all over the place, and you say... "next leg,
please." Rimbaud is like being stabbed with a pitchfork a
thousand million times... until you smile. Where are you
from?

BITSY: Greenwich, Connecticut.

JOAQUÍN: No! You come from the inner recesses of my imagination. A wondrous place, a magical place, a most sacred
place.

BITSY: (*Incredulously.*) Greenwich, Connecticut?

JOAQUÍN: Yes! What's your name?

BITSY: Bitsy.

JOAQUÍN: Bitsy, Bitsy, Bitsy... bits of suffering, bits of
anguish, bits of nothingness.

BITSY: Bitsy Jones.

JOAQUÍN: (*Extending his hand.*) Joaquín Bucaramanga at
your service. (*He takes her hand and starts kissing his
way up the arm.*) What an interesting limb you've
got... Bitsy.

BITSY: Why, thank you.

JOAQUÍN: This hand tells me many stories. This finger, for
example, belonged to a Nubian princess. Many people
handed you things, and you... you... handed them back.

BITSY: Ohhh. I like that.

JOAQUÍN: And this finger belonged to a three-hundred pound monk who tormented himself to death and was joyous ever after.

BITSY: Ohhhhh...I've always had a weight problem.

JOAQUÍN: And this finger...this finger belongs to me. (*He starts sucking her little finger, she is enraptured.*) My God, Bitsy. Look. Your hair. You have the most exquisitely tormented hair I've ever seen. You will torment me, we will torment each other. You know Rimbaud?

BITSY: Uh?

JOAQUÍN: You know nothingness?!

BITSY: Well...

JOAQUÍN: Of course, you do! And what is Art? Art was the Pyramids. And why did they build the Pyramids?

BITSY: Hotels?

JOAQUÍN: I never thought of that. It's a sign. I live in a hotel. I believe in signs. I'm from San Juan, Puerto Rico.

BITSY: (*Enchanted.*) Oh my god! You're a real Puerto Rican?

JOAQUÍN: It goes without saying. Bitsy, why don't you come downtown to my space.

BITSY: I'm not that kind of girl.

JOAQUÍN: But you could be. We will make little poesies together. We will eat little nothings and starve and wither away in each others arms until we're dried and desiccated.

BITSY: Ick!

JOAQUÍN: Bitsy, don't be like this. This moment was prewritten in time...before I was interesting.

BITSY: Oh, I think you're very interesting now.

JOAQUÍN: Come away with me. Come! Use your imagination! Fly away from this miserable place. We'll fly downtown. (*Leaps, attempting to fly.*) Fly! Fly! Fly! Bitsy, you're my left wing...you're not flying! (*He falls to the ground and embraces her knees, crestfallen.*) I love you, Bitsy.

BITSY: This is really neat, but...

JOAQUÍN: Well how about it?

BITSY: (*Completely torn.*) I have to catch the 5:05.

JOAQUÍN: 5:05, interesting concept, 5:05. I get the five on this side, and I understand the five on this side. But this thing in the middle doesn't make any sense to me.

BITSY: It's a zero.

JOAQUÍN: Zero! Don't you want to starve and wither like desiccated lovers?

BITSY: No. I have to meet my mother at the country club for dinner.

JOAQUÍN: Can I join you?

BITSY: (*Horrified.*) No! (*She runs stage left.*)

JOAQUÍN: Bitsy, don't leave me. I'll just sit here and let my atoms disperse into the atmosphere. (*Reading.*) Hell is eternal torment.

Music swells up as autumn leaves fall.

Menudo

Lights change and the music of the singing group, Menudo, comes up as Rick *becomes a Menudo-teen idol.* Luisa *(Stage left.) and* Diane *(Stage right.) enter as make-up girls. The girls begin to primp* Menudo *for his performance.* Menudo *begins to lip sync his hit song, microphone in hand. Girls exit screaming stage left.* Armando *enters stage left as restaurant manager and hands* Rick *his coffee pot, scalding his hand. The flashback is shattered. Lights change and we are at the restaurant where he is currently employed.*

MANAGER: Use the handle next time, Raúl. It's much smarter. (*Grabs* Mike.) Ramírez party of twelve, your table is ready. Thank you very much.

RICK: (Rick *stands, looks around softly. Music plays softly in the background as he walks from table to table. At one table he insists the pot of coffee is caffeinated. At the next, he says, "Don't worry it's decaf." He walks like an old man, not the nineteen-year old that he is. Arthritis has taken its toll on this once-proud teen idol.*) It's decaf. Decaf. Swear to God, decaf. Did you want caffeinated. It's caffeinated. Caffeinated. Swear to God, caffeinated. Yeah, I used to be somebody. I had lots of money, cars, girls, everything an adolescent boy could want. I wanted to be the best, the greatest, the Latin Michael Jackson, but darker, and with less plastic surgery. Yeah, I made a lot of money in my time. I was in Menudo. Menudo, oh Menudo. (*He dances as he says the words, spilling coffee on a customer.*) Sorry. Sorry. (*He does a feeble dance move recalled from deep in his memory.*)

Those were the happiest times of my life. I was just an innocent twelve-year old when I joined. But they kick you out when you turn seventeen. I was the only idiot who gave my real age. (*He launches into the Menudo move and stops.*) Ay, Menudo, Menudo, Menudo. Life was great back then. My manger invested my money in great things: clothes, motorcycles, RV's, CD's, his house, his bank accounts, his mutual funds, his IRA's. But I ain't got no regrets. *Ay,* Menudo...Menudo, Menudo! (*Spills coffee.*) Sorry. Sorry.

And I remember it so clearly. One day, my manager came in with this *mocoso* punk kid. And the kid said, "Who's the old man?" And I realized he was talking about me. Me! And then, it was over, *se acabó,* just like the Vikki Carr song, but even more dramatic. *Ay,* Menudo, Menudo. Uh, there goes my back. (*His back and pelvis give out.*) But I ain't got no regrets. I can take it. Hell, I'm only nineteen. I've got my whole life ahead of me in the wonderful food-service industry. I was left with a lot of great memories and shot vocal cords and varicose veins and pelvic arthritis. Classic P.M.S.S.- Post Menudo Shock Syndrome.

And whenever somebody says to me, "Didn't you used to be somebody?", I say, "Hey pal, I am somebody!" (*He sees a girl in the audience and addresses her.*) Yeah, you recognize me, you must read Tiger Beat. No, I ain't Donny

Osmond. He works down the street at Denny's! Yeah. (*Menudo music comes up.*) I used to be somebody. I used to be somebody. I *am* somebody. (*Throws a kiss.*)

Lights slowly fade out.

Meeting 3

DIANE: (*Enters carrying two cups of coffee.*) Okay. All right, who wanted the cappuccino royale with the mint expresso and the caffe latte with the banana swirl? Well, all you get is black coffee, so get over it. (*Hands one cup of coffee to* Armando *and the other to an audience member.*) People, people, you have to put money in the donation box. It's getting real low. OH! OH! OH! (REFERRING TO AN AUDIENCE MEMBER) Your share last week...it really affected me. The program really works.

ARMANDO: (*To same audience member.*) Yeah. Great share. Can you just go over that one more time for everyone here.

DIANE: Just relive the moment. (*Encouraging.*) You know...The Chicano Moratorium...Rubén Salazar Park 1970...over twenty-five years ago. Can't you remember? I really related to it. I used to be a member of the vanguard of the Chicano Movement. I used to shout "Chicano Power!" "*¡Que Viva La Raza!*" "*¡Sí se puede!*" "*¡No nos moverán!*" "*¡Que viva César Chávez!*" "Oh, *bella ciao, bella ciao, bella ciao, ciao, ciao!*" Now, the strange thing is...I don't speak Spanish. I've always faked it real well because that's the kind of commitment you need. A lot of people would ask me, "What kind of Chicana are you? You, a conscious person, a member of the vanguard of the Chicano Movement?" Hey man, don't question my commitment. Being a Chicano is a state of mind. Being a Chicano is the hope for the future. Being a Chicano is...a lot of fuckin' work. All right. I admit it. I just want a Jeep Cherokee. I want a house in Newport Beach, and an Anglo gardener. God, I'm sounding like a broken record...Diane, Chicana Ranasaurus Rex! (Armando *jumps up. He urges the audience to applaud* Diane's *share.*)

ARMANDO: (*Trying to comfort her.*) What a great share! But, Diane, to be Chicana Ranasaurus Rex and not speak your own language... The shame, the humiliation, the ignorance...

DIANE: Armando, you are such an insensitive macho idiot!

ARMANDO: Thank you. (*Doesn't know what he said wrong.*) I guess I'll share. Hi, my name is Armando (*Waits for audience response.*) Thanks. Insensitive macho idiot. Hey, I'm working on it. Like last night, I went to a female mud-wrestling show and I let her pin me. I still drive my red Trans Am with the turbo jet rocket thrusters on the side—sometimes fire comes out of them—when I'm in the mood. Seriously, I am working on it. This is my 45th month coming to these meetings, and this is my first time sharing. Thanks, um, yesterday I had a regression, no, more like a past life experience. Well, I guess I just had a memory. I remembered when I was nine-years old. I was at Coney Island and my mom would call me over. "*M'ijo, m'ijo,*" she'd say. That means my son in Spanish, for you Anglo co-dependents. "You'd better get out of the sun because you're gonna get too dark." So she put on the highest sunscreen lotion, number 52, and that zinc oxide stuff. I looked like Casper the friendly ghost with brown spots coming through. I realized, through primal therapy, (we call it primal *grito* here), why she was so afraid of me getting dark. I remember we took this summer vacation from New York to Florida. We stopped in North Carolina to get something to eat. We walked into this sleazy diner making this big *revolu* in Spanish. (*Rattling off.*) "*Que esto, que el otro, que sé yo.*" And this big guy said to us (*Imitates guy cocking gun.*), "We don't serve Puerto Ricans here." And my brother said, "We're not Puerto Rican. We're Colombian."

Blackout.

Latch Key Kids

Bright mariachi music plays. Mother *enters dressed in her "Beauty Bucket Salon" uniform and beehive hair-do. She carries a bag of groceries.*

MOTHER: *Ay, viejo* hurry up. *Ay,* what a day. (*Puts groceries down.*)

FATHER: (Father *enters dressed as a mechanic, carrying some lotto tickets.*) If you'd let me play lotto more often, we could get out of here instead of us both working all week. You should be home with the kids. It ain't natural.

MOTHER: Do you think I like working at the Beauty Bucket? We need the money. *Ay,* you and your lottery. No one wins.

FATHER: Mexicans and Pakistani 7-Eleven guys always win. I'm gonna pick a winner someday.

MOTHER: The only thing you know how to pick is a good wife.

FATHER: *Ay, vieja.*

MOTHER: *Viejo.*

FATHER: *Vieja.* (*They snuggle together. He rubs his hands on her cheek.*)

MOTHER: *Ay,* your hands are greasy. And besides, the kids are home.

FATHER: *¡Ay!* Those kids. I'm tired of working two jobs to keep up with the Montoya's.

MOTHER: You have to. They got a new big-screen T.V. and a Cutlass Supreme.

FATHER: *Ay,* what do you expect? He's a drug dealer!

MOTHER: *¡Ay!* You think everyone who's Latino and rich is a drug dealer. He's a pharmacist.

FATHER: *Ay,* same thing!

MOTHER: *Ay,* same thing! Here put these away.

FATHER: *Ay, mandona. (Bossy)*

MOTHER: *Ayyyyy.* María, Juan, we're home! (*Two kids come out dressed as punk rockers with shaved heads and Mohawks.* Juan *and* María *start to sing.*)

JUAN: (*Singing.*) I just wanna be an American. Don't you?

MARÍA: (*Singing.*) Don't want no nationality but American. Don't you?

JUAN: (*Singing.*) I just want to be free to watch my MTV.

MARÍA: (*Singing.*) I just want to play with my pink hair.

JUAN and MARÍA: (*Singing.*) American Aryan. American Aryan. American Aryan. American Aryan.

FATHER: Aryan!? You're Mexican!

JUAN and MARÍA: Yeah, we're Mexican. Not!

MOTHER: Why are you kids dressed like this?

JUAN and MARÍA: Like what?

MOTHER: Like "Nightmare on (*Local.*) Street."

MARÍA: We've been dressing like this for six months.

JUAN: This is permanent! (Juan *and* María *do the Bark.*)

FATHER: If your *abuelo* was alive, he'd drop dead, *cabrones*!!!

JUAN and MARÍA: Speak English, dude!

MOTHER: *Ay,* after everything we've given you kids!

JUAN and MARÍA: Except time! (*They exit up stage left.*)

FATHER: What about your *quinceañera*?

MOTHER: They've become...

MOTHER and FATHER: Latch key kids! (Mother *sings* ay's *to the tune of* "La Paloma," Father *speaks words between each of* Mother's *lines.*)

MOTHER: *Ay, ay, ay, ay, ay...*

FATHER: ...If only there was a day care.

MOTHER: *Ay, ay, ay, ay, ay...*

FATHER: ...If only we could afford it.

MOTHER: *Ay, ay, ay, ay, ay...*

FATHER: ...Those kids are driving me crazy.

MOTHER: *Ay, ay, ay, ay, ay...*

FATHER: ...Shut up already!

MOTHER: *Ay, ay, ay, ay, ay*
Ay, ay, ay, ay, ay

Ay, ay, ay, ay, ay
Paloma!

Mother and Father hold each other as lights dim.

Meeting 4

Nicolette *appears silhouetted against back wall, singing*
"La vie en rose." Lights up. Nicolette *breaks down, tries to pick*
up the song again and breaks down again.

NICOLETTE: *Au revoir*, Nicolette, *au revoir.*

ALL: *Au revoir*, Nicolette.

NICOLETTE: *(She resumes her song, takes off beret and dark*
  glasses.) I am not Française. All zeeze monz I've been
  coming 'ere, I've been lying... about everything. My name
  is Luisa, just plain Luisa. And I've never been to Monte
  Carlo. I'm from Guatemala.

RICK: Bummer.

NICOLETTE: "A backward country"—Guatemala. "What part
  of Mexico is that? Say something in Guatemalan..."
  (Searching.) "Yankee Imperialist go home?" As a kid I
  was mortified to be from Guatemala. There has never
  been anyone internationally famous from Guatemala. I
  would bug my mom for hours at a time, "Mom, please tell
  me I'm adopted!" I wasn't. I was nine when we moved to
  the States and that's when I decided to never speak Spanish again, and to change my name from Luisa Josefina
  Gómez to Nicolette Sauvignon Blanc.

  I'm really trying to work the program, so... *(Strug-*
  gling.) I admit I'm La...La... I admit I'm La...La... I'm
  really Russian you know? For real. It's not even a lie. My
  mom's Russian. So that makes me half-Russian. Techni-
  cally, I don't even have to be at these meetings. I mean,
  what's so great about being Latin anyway? *(There is an*
  awkward pause as Nicolette *ends her share.)*

ALL: *(Recovering.)* Breakthrough! *(They clap.)*

RICK: What an incredible share! A Guata-Russian? (*Upset,* Luisa/Nicolette *runs off stage.*) Did I say something wrong?

ARMANDO: You know those Guata-Russians... They make good red sauce!

DIANE: Yeah, I'd be French, too, if I was from Guatemala. By the way, Rick, did you ever find the dues money?

RICK: (*As he exits.*) No, I'm still looking.

ARMANDO: (*To audience.*) Wasn't there a Guatemalan who won the Nobel Prize? (*Gets audience member to answer, "Rigoberto Menchu."*) Rigoberta Menchu! (*Running off.*) Nicolette, uh, Luisa! There's hope for your people yet!

Blackout.

Separate Turf

We hear the pounding rhythm of rap music, two gangs, one Mexican and the other Puerto Rican, appear on stage. They circle each other menacingly, snapping their fingers a la "West Side Story." It builds into a crescendo with the men flashing gang hand signals using the vowels a.e.i.o.u.

MEX CHANO: Hey, what are you doing here?

P.R. CHANO: No, what are you doing here?

MEX CHANO: No, what are you doing here?

P.R. CHANO: No, what are you doing here?

MEX MARÍA: Eh, *vatos,* cut it out! Let me handle this! (*The two girls take center stage.*) Hey, what are you doing here?

P.R. MARÍA: No, what are you doing here?

MEX MARÍA: No, what are you doing here?

P.R. MARÍA: No, what are you doing here?

MEX MARÍA: No, *cabrona,* what are you doing here?

P.R. MARÍA: *A mí no me llaman cabrona.* (*They go at each other in classic spitfire tradition: lots of hair pulling, kicking and screaming, "cabrona," "pendeja," etc. The two guys pull them apart. The men go into flashing signs again.*

CHINO/CHANO: A. E. I. O. U. (*Flashing gangland hand signals.*)

MEX CHANO: This ain't your barrio, *vato*. You know your territory. We got a truce, man. We don't want no trouble, but if you start it, we'll end it.

P.R. CHINO: Hey mang, how'd you hear about this audition?

MEX CHANO: Same way you did...in the streets.

P.R. CHINO: *Coño, mang*. I heard about it through the Hollywood Reporter.

MEX CHANO: Hollywood Reporter? You're East Coast *vato*!

P.R. CHINO: Hey, Regional Theatre is neutral turf, bro.

MEX CHANO: Bullshit, you've got Broadway and Off Broadway and Off Off Broadway.

P.R. CHINO: Listen, mang! They haven't done a "West Side Story" revival in years!

P.R. MARÍA: We've got a right to sell out and go Hollywood too, you know!

MEX CHANO: Hey, half the so-called Chicano roles in Hollywood are played by Cubans and Puerto (SPIT) Ricans.

P.R. MARÍA: That's because we can overact! (*They all four enter into a spitting contest, ending with the women threatening to spit a big one from the deepest part of throats.*)

MEX CHANO: Hey, cut that out! Act like ladies. (*The men quickly go back to their own confrontation, flashing gang signs—A.E.I.O.U.*)

P.R. CHINO: There ain't enough roles to go around, *coño*. (*The two men assume a fighting stance.*)

MEX CHANO: Then you better back off, man, I got a three-octave range.

P.R. MARÍA: Watch it, Chino. He's trained. (Mex Chano *lets out a* grito.)

MEX COUPLE: (*Singing and dancing to "Cielito lindo."*)
Ay, ay, ay, ay,
I like to work cheap
I'll play a thief, a pimp, or a creep

As long as it's on Hill Street.

P.R. COUPLE: We can do better than that. (*They take center stage and start singing and dancing to "I Want to Live in America."*)

I like to act in America.

Hokay by me in America!

I'll play a maid in America!

Stereotype in America! *¡Ole!*

(*They milk the audience for applause.*)

MEX CHANO: Don't encourage those Puerto Ricans. I hate bad musical theater! (*Pulling out a knife.*)

P.R. MARÍA: Watch out, Chino, he's got a knife! (P.R. Chino *pulls out a gun.*)

MEX MARÍA: Watch it, Chano, he's got a gun! (*A slow-motion death dance ensues. The girls, screaming, also move in slow motion.*)

P.R. CHINO: *Coño*, eat this. (*He shoots gun and* Mex Chano *stabs him.*) Oh, shit.

MEX CHANO: Oh, no! (*They both fall dead.*)

MEX MARÍA: Oh, no, Chano!

P.R. MARÍA: Oh, no, Chino! (*The women try to one-up each other.*)

MEX MARÍA: Oh, no, Chano!

P.R. MARÍA: Oh, no, Chino!

MEX MARÍA: Oh, no, Chano!

P.R. MARÍA: Okay, you win! (*She throws herself violently on* Chino.)

MEX MARÍA: (*Satisfied with her performance, she picks up the gun.*) Are there enough bullets for you, Chano? And for you... Cochino! And you?... You... What's your name?

P.R. MARÍA: What do you think it is?

ALL: (*Singing.*) María.

MEX MARÍA: For you, María? Or the producers or the casting directors or the network heads? We have to stop this senseless gang violence. You stick to Broadway and Off Broadway, we'll stick to Equity Waiver and Regional Theatre, even if it means we'll starve waiting for (*Local the-atre.*) to cast us. And you on the East Coast, pray for that "West Side Story" revival, and pray Natalie Wood doesn't rise from the grave. You'll take "America's Most Wanted," and we'll take occasional episodes of "Highway Patrol," or "Cops," now that "Hill Street" is gone. And we'll split all the bit parts... There will be a lot of those.... (*During the latter part of her speech,* P.R. María, *not to be outdone, starts sobbing very melodramatically.*)

P.R. MARÍA: (P.R. María *genuflects.*) ¡Ay dios mio! What have we done?!

MEX MARÍA: Shut up! You're upstaging me!!! (*She shoots her,* P.R. María *milks her death.*) Amateur! And please, *carnales*, let's try to love one another and live in peace.

VOICE OVER: (*Voice over of the* Casting Director *is heard from the house.*) Fine, fine, kids. But can you do it with heavier accent?

ALL: Heavier accent!

RICK: It doesn't get any heavier than this!

ARMANDO: I need a job.

DIANE: I need an image.

LUISA: I need a break

ALL: Intermission.

Blackout.

Act Two

Meeting 5

We hear a loud rendition of "La Marcha de Zacatecas." Armando, Rick *and* Luisa *enter from audience, throwing Mexican gritos and clapping, urging the audience to join in. The music stops as* Armando *steps forward.*)

ARMANDO: That's great. What a great group. That was almost special. So... let's try what I call the collective *grito*. On three. Everyone. One. Two. Three. (*All throw a* grito.) Let's do it again, but with more *huevos*.

RICK: Yeah, more *huevos rancheros*.

ARMANDO: Okay. Everyone, *uno*, *dos*, three.

RICK: That was great. Now, for you Anglos who want to really experience a *grito*, just put your hand in a car door and slam it. Then you'll feel the pain and suffering of our people. (*To the others*.) Announcements?

ARMANDO: We're taking reservations for the whitewater rafting trip down the East L.A. River. Be sure to wear your sunscreen. Should be lots of fun.

LUISA: And Guadalupe gave birth last night to a healthy eighteen-pound baby boy. Little Maclovio. Natural childbirth.

RICK: Wow, now that's a real *grito*. On a more serious note; we've noticed some hesitancy from you newcomers to get up and share—especially you Anglo co-dependents. So, as we say in Fresno, let's just pick an Anglo. (*He scans the audience for an Anglo*.) You. Why don't you stand. What's you're name? (*If Anglo gives a Latin name,* Rick's *lines are,* "We are trained councilors. We know you are in Anglo denial. What do they call you at home?")

ALL: Hi, _____.

RICK: You know, it takes a lot of courage to get up and share something very personal, especially with people you've never met before. I admire your courage. So... could you just stand up and share something *very* personal from the Anglo experience. Come on, let's give him a big hand. (*The rest of the cast adlibs encouragements to get the Anglo co-dependent to share*.)

DIANE: (*Rushes in*.) I'm late. I'm late. I'm really, really late. I'm sorry. Let's get the meeting started...

LUISA: Diane, it's already started. _____ was about to share.

DIANE: How could you start without me?

RICK: I didn't think you were coming, and _____ was in a lot of Anglo angst.

DIANE: When have I not come to a meeting?

ARMANDO: It's okay, Diane, _____ is going to share any second now.

DIANE: It's not okay! We always start on Latino time! Now, I have this petition I want everyone to sign it. It's to "Save the (*Local reference.*)"

RICK: Not another petition. We don't have time. Poor _____ wants to stand up and share. GET UP!

DIANE: _____, can you give me a minute? Sit down. Don't have time? What kind of people are you?

RICK: We are people who are trying to have a meeting. (*Turns to Anglo co-dependent.*) _____, get up and share.

DIANE: You know, I sense a little hostility here. I've had therapy. I can take it. So I'm going to leave. (*To Anglo co-dependent.*) _____ can fucking share if he wants to. I'm sure there's a meeting somewhere that needs me. (Armando *and* Luisa *offer their apologies to the Anglo co-dependent for* Diane.)

ARMANDO: We're really sorry, _____. It must be the Mexican-American war thing.

LUISA: He's going to be in therapy for years.

DIANE: (*Frantically searching through her purse.*) Where is my day planner? (*Accusing Anglo co-dependent*) _____? (Rick *stops her.*) Somebody stole my day planner. Who had the motive? Who had the most to gain? The ability to cover up? My God, it's a plot. The C.I.A. stole my day planner! Check the grassy knoll!! Check the doors. The C.I.A. stole my day planner!

RICK: (RICK *pulls out a bell and rings.*) Diane, calm down, calm down, Diane.

DIANE: (*Screams at* Rick.) What are you doing with my bell? I'm the leader.

RICK: Diane! We take turns leading here.

DIANE: What is this, a coup? I'm the elected president. You're
just the treasurer.

RICK: According to our constitution, the leader can change
when the membership so decrees! (*To audience.*) Am I
right, people?

DIANE: NO! No! I'm not stepping down, you conniving cheat!
What did you do with the dues money?

RICK: Those were only allegations. Nothing was ever proved.

DIANE: Ha!

RICK: I'll get back your dues money, people. Just give me a
little time, _____, stop looking at me. (*Referring to
Anglo co-dependent.*) You never paid a dime. The people
will follow me, Diane.

DIANE: No! they'll follow me!

RICK: No! The people will follow me, Diane. (*Referring to
Anglo co-dependent.*) _____, follow me! (Diane *and*
Rick *exit.* Luisa *and* Armando *let the moment set in.*)

ARMANDO: Who are you going to follow?

LUISA: I don't know. They're both so charismatic.
Blackout.

Hermana Petra

VOICE OVER STAGE MANAGER: Standing by. On cue. Five,
four, three, two, one. GO! (*A very local cable TV station
stage. A smarmy producer type comes out and announces.*)

M.C.: And now, ladies and gentlemen's, broadcasting live from
la calle Third and Broadway. The talk show host of host-
esses. The woman with an opinion and a bunion, that
glamour gal, the woman behind la Virgen de Guadalupe,
Dos Equis presents everyones *comadre*...La Hermana
Petra!!!!! (Petra *enters,* M.C. *flashes applause sign.*)

PETRA: *Gracias, gracias, gracias, señores, señoras, y los que
quedan.* I can't tell you how popular the show is getting.
Your letters have been pouring in and your telephone
calls have been jamming the lines. Son of a bitchi, I'm a

hit. *La* Oprah better watch out, I'm going to take over. *Ay, Ay, Ay.* Oh *m'ijos*. Call me. I can help. I don't mean to brag, but you know la Chata Gonzales...*la gordita* from down the street?... I gave her some of my special 'anti-cellulite' teas, for $9.99 plus tax, and her thighs are melting away like my Tupperware when I leave it on the stove. *Es un milagro*, it's a miracle. (M.C. *flashes applause sign, then send-money sign.*) *Hermanitos*, you are all too kind. You know how the show works, especially during pledge week. I ask for a very small donation. (M.C. *flashes applause sign and send-money sign.*) If we do not receive your donation within ten days, one of my producers will come a calling. (M.C. *flashes bat.*) And now for the calls. First caller, you're on the air.

CALLER #1: (*We hear voice over of heavy breathing.*)

PETRA: Not, now, José! I'm working. *Ay*, husbands. We have an audience member who wants to ask us a question. I love the dress. Where did you get it? *La* Penney?

WOMAN: (Luisa *as* Woman *walks on stage.*) Sí.

PETRA: What is your question?

WOMAN: Please don't tell no one, but I haven't been able to get pregnant.

PETRA: Well, are you on the pill?

WOMAN: Yes.

PETRA: Then get off it.

WOMAN: I never thought of that, *ay*, *Hermana*, you are a medical genius.

PETRA: *Gracias*, *m'ija*. Next caller. You're on the air.

CALLER #2: *Hermana*, this is Airman basic Pete García

PETRA: Sí, Basic Airman Pete...

CALLER #2: I'm working in Omaha, Nebraska, at a missile silo. There's two buttons and I pushed them. The missile's ready to launch. I'm going to lose my job and all of Eastern Europe!

PETRA: Pete, don't panic. It's probably just a 22 megaton warhead. Process down and translate at a rate of 12.999

b.s.'s. You got that, Pete? And for Pete's sake, if that doesn't work...unplug the *chingadera*.

CALLER #2: Hey, that unplugging works. You're an aeronautical genius!

PETRA: *Ay*, you people really need me. (*Crossing up to platform.*) Next caller, you're on the air.

ARMANDO: Hello, Hermana. This is Armando.

PETRA: Armandito, did you get the tamales I sent you?

ARMANDO: Oh, is that what they were? Listen, Hermanita, I finally shared at the Latins Anonymous meeting.

PETRA: Excellent, *m'ijo*, excellent.

ARMANDO: But I have a new problem.

PETRA: What is it, *m'ijo*?

ARMANDO: Women. I just don't understand women.

PETRA: Oooooh, Armando. I'm good, but I'm not that good. The problem with women is that they get excited about nothing and then they marry him. But, *m'ijo*...keep trying. There's still hope.

ARMANDO: Oh, thank you, Hermana. You're a psychosomatic genius.

PETRA: *Ay*, *m'ijo*, what a compliment. Oh, I see I'm getting the red light. Join me next week for my show, "Hispanics in Hollywood and the Italians who play them." *Gracias, m'ijos, gracias.*

Lights fade on Petra.

Machos of Omaha

VOICE OVER: Welcome to yet another episode of "Macho of Omaha's Wild Kingdom." Machos...(*Toreador music blares, and we see two men walk on stage. The men strut around the stage and finally strike various macho-men poses.*)

JUAN: (*Exposes a small amount of chest hair proudly to the audience.*) Welcome to "Macho of Omaha's Wild Kingdom."

I am the one and only Juan Valdez, and this is my co-host, Fidel Castro.

FIDEL: Our audience was sick and tired of seeing grown men wrestle with anaconadas and tag and weigh puny little endangered species, because who is more endangered? Us, los Machos. (Fidel strikes Juan.)

JUAN: Where's Ernest Hemingway?

FIDEL: Humphrey Bogart?

JUAN: James Cagney?

FIDEL: Tony Montana?

JUAN: Juan Wayne? Gone. That's where. And who's left? Sylvester Stallone. He's a pussy.

FIDEL: Arnold Schwartzenneger, pussy, pussy.

JUAN: Chuck Norris, pussy, pussy, pussy.

FIDEL: Oprah Winfrey. *(He hesitates.)*

BOTH: No, she's pretty tough.

JUAN: Now let's show our adoring studio audience our Macho travels before my testosterone levels get so high... I get so angry that I kill someone. *(Pulls hair off his chest.)*

FIDEL: Don't worry. It'll grow back in an hour.

BOTH: Roll film, Bruno! *(EFX: Film rolling and lights flickering.)*

JUAN: Here's an oldie but goodie! Here's Fidel wrestling and tagging soldiers in El Salvador. I bet that high altitude in the beautiful mountains of El Salvador slowed you down a bit, didn't it?

FIDEL: Just a little. We tagged and weighed that Salvadoran officer. He came in at two hundred ninety-nine pounds.

JUAN: Must be all that good ol' American Aid.

FIDEL: Roll film, Bruno! Now, here we are in Miami, Florida, talking to our favorite macho, Manuel Noriega. There he is with his court-appointed attorneys from Jacoby and Meyers. Tell me, Juan, how did you lure Manny to our Macho cameras?

JUAN: That was easy. I just said, "Hey, Manny, I got your ex-dermatologist over here. Want to talk to him? Boy, did he want to talk to his ex-dermatologist.

BOTH: Wango, wango.

JUAN: The old cattle prod.

FIDEL: Okay, roll the film, Bruno!

JUAN: Stop rolling the film! The only thing short on a macho is his attention span.

BOTH: Think about it. *(To the audience.)* They did.

JUAN: Okay. Let's take some questions from our adoring studio audience.

BOTH: Vanita! Vanita Blanca. *(Vanita, every macho male's dream bimbo, enters. She picks a man from the audience.)*

VANITA: Machos, this is a man from Vienna, Juan and the only Valdez. His name is Giuseppi and he sings castrata with the Viennese Boys Choir. He wants to know if he can be a macho.

BOTH: No! Next question.

VANITA: This man says his wife beats him and forces him to wear her clothes and stay home and have children. Can he be a macho?

BOTH: No!!!

JUAN: But she can.

VANITA: Fidel, this is a question for you from this man from West Hollywood. And he wants to know why you don't call him anymore.

FIDEL: Hey! Hey! Hey! Hey! Hey! Hey! Hey! Stop the show! *(To man in audience.)* I swear I have never seen that man. *(Then to Juan.)* I can't stand a man who kisses and tells. Next question.

VANITA: *(Approaches beautiful woman.)* This *caliente* number says machos turn her on and she's in town for a few days for the National Rifle Association convention. She wants to know what's the most macho thing you have done.

JUAN: Let me answer that.

FIDEL: No, let me answer that. *(The machos ram each other with their chests and Juan wins.)*

JUAN: Ahh, *querida*, and I do mean *querida*. One of the most macho things I did was run with the bulls of Pamplona, and after being gored several times throughout my macho steroid-infested body, I finished the race two hours ahead of those puny bulls.

FIDEL: That's nothing, women's work. I ran with the starving pit bulls of East L.A. I ran with hunks of meat tied around my neck. Now, that's macho!

JUAN: Nothing, little girls in pink tights with asthma work. I went to a cock fight and didn't even bring a rooster. I killed that bird.

FIDEL: Oh, yeah. That's little girls in pink tutus in the "Nutcracker Suite" work. I...I...I castrated myself with my own teeth to prove to a woman that I loved her.

JUAN: *(Stops unable to answer.)* Wow, that's really macho.

VANITA: That's really stupid. *(She exits.)*

FIDEL: A real macho is a great liar! *(They shake hands as music comes up. They grab their folding chairs and close them simultaneously, castrating themselves. As they exit, they wave to the audience.)*

BOTH: Good night, everybody.

Blackout.

Lolana Aerobics

To the sounds of driving rock music, Lolana crosses behind a scrim, doing jumping jacks, leg raises, etc. She is heard encouraging her class. "Three more! Feel the burn! Two more! Last one." She limps on stage, exhausted.

LOLANA: *(Calling off-stage.)* Good workout, girls! See you next week. Bye, Debbie, bye, Susie, bye, Buffy! *(To audience.)* *Ay*, those *gringa* workouts, they want to lose ten pounds in one hour! *Hola, chicas!* Welcome to Lolana aerobics! I'm Lolana and, ooh, I'm feeling good. Okay! *(She*

removes aerobic shoes and puts on spike heels in prepara-
tion for her class.)

This is the Advanced Latin Woman's aerobics class where we exercise our femininity. And, *chicas,* don't let anybody kid you, femininity does not come natural, uh, uh, it takes technique! For today's class, our focus is going to be on...*men!* Oh, I like that! Okay! When you see a man you want, *chicas,* you've got to be like a heat-seeking missile. *(She picks a man and slinks over.)*

Hi. I know you're a man. Oh, I like that. Will you love Lolana? *(Pause.)* You see? Dead silence. Why? Because I'm using bad technique. You can't ask a man to love you, you've got to *inspire* him to love you. So, okay, *chicas!* Let's inspire! We're going to warm up our most lethal weapon...our hips! *(Shaking her hips like maracas.)* A Latina's hips know no rest. They work 24 hours a day. Dusting. *(Sings Santana's "Oye como va.")* Standing still. *Amorcito,* will you zip me up? When you're steamed! *¡Coño! (Vigorously bounces from side to side with hand on hip.)*

See this backward and forward movement? Really good for when you're mad. Feeling mad!

Okay, *chicas!* Let's take a little breather. *(Wiping her brow with towel.)* Remember, we do not want to exercise too vigorously. If God had meant us to be skinny, he would have made us *gringas!* Let's do our first combination. For you busy career women, you can even do this in the office! First, you target a male. *You! (Walks over to the man and drops the towel all innocent.) Ay, se me cayó.*

Hips, remember, a good Latina has no sharp angles. Now you bend over and you pick it up. See what a nice fanny lift you get? See what a nice view *you* get. *(Indicating audi-ence member.)* And for you, *chicas,* who prefer to work with cleavage, it's just a minor adjustment. *(Turns around and shows as much bossom as possible.)* See? Ooh, feeling good. Okay, *chicas,* let's put it all together. This is very advanced, so don't strain yourselves. "Ay, se me cayó." *(Drops Towel.)* No, honey. I'll pick it up. Ohh, you're such a strong man. *(In a deep plié.)* See how I'm looking up at the man? See how big and important it makes him feel? See how I'm toning up my thighs? Now, try to hold down there for as long as you possibly can. No pain, no gain! Three, two, one! *Ay,* okay, walk it out! Walk it out! Shake it out! Remember, being feminine means suffering, just a little bit.

This was a good workout, girls. Next week, we're going to make housework work for you. I'll teach you how to keep your man steaming hot while pumping iron. *(She pretends to iron.)* Feeling good! *(She dances off.)*

ARMANDO: (Armando *enters truly moved, sympathetic and exhausted by what he's seen* Lolana *go through.)* Whew! That's a lot of work! I mean, I just never realized how tough it is...what women GO through!... You guys, you guys, listen up. Women have gotten the short end of the stick, and I've had it! I've changed! I've read "Men are from Mars, women are from Venus." I jog with women who run with the wolves. *(To man from meeting five.)* As an Anglo co-dependent, I'm sure you can understand. You've gotta get this book. I went back to school and got a degree in Women's Studies from Vassar! And I've started to go to other meetings..."Women, Sex and Power" meetings..."Women in Film" seminars, OA meetings, Seasonal Color Analysis workshops. I have *two* cats!

You see, I work on my relationship with women daily because that's the kind of commitment it takes. I volunteer at Lamaze classes. I'm studying to be a midwife. I take Midol to get high. Because I understand. I've had the Cinderella Complex, the Wendy Syndrome, and I even know where Tinkerbell was coming from. I want to share, I want to nurture. I want to listen, but I also want to be heard.

I want to be supportive, and sensitive but strong and independent. And I want my partner to be supportive and sensitive, yet strong and independent, too. And I never fall
asleep after sex, never...God...after sex I can't fall asleep
for days! Because I hear the biological clock of every
woman in the world ticking in my ears. And I...I want to
experience childbirth...I want to bleed!!!!! *(Doubles over
in pain.)*
Oh, I think I've got cramps.

Blackout.

Calvino De Kline

(A television parody of an effete perfume commercial.)

VOICE OVER: "Machos of Omaha" is brought to you by Calvino De Kline's "Obnoxious." Oh, the smell of it! *(Over a bed
of new-age music a cacophony of voices is heard whisper-
ing dramatic nothings: "I want you," "I need you," "Oh the
pain of it." The following is done in a choreographed
dance of self-consciousness.)*
DIANE: Liars.
ARMANDO AND RICK: Lovers not liars.
RICK: Calvino de Kline's "Obnoxious."
LUISA: *(Running across stage.)* Happiness...laughter...*mari-
posas.* HA! HA! HA ! HA!
DIANE: *Así era tu mundo.*
ARMANDO: *Angustias...gritos...el tuyo*
DIANE: *El tuyo.*
ARMANDO: *¡Tuyo!*
DIANE: *¡Tuyo!*
ARMANDO: *¡Tu!*
DIANE: *¡Tu! (Rick slaps Diane, Diane slaps Rick, Rick slaps
Armando, They all look at Luisa.)*

LUISA: *(Slaps herself. Laughs and runs away.)* Ha! Ha! Ha!
   Ha!

RICK: "Obnoxious." I wanted her like the moon wants water.

DIANE: Her hurt knew no pain. *(Luisa Slaps Rick.)*

RICK: "Obnoxious."

LUISA: HA! HA! HA! HA!

ARMANDO: Her laughter was like broken butterflies.

ALL: ¡Olvídarte! ¡Jamás!

ARMANDO: *(Seeing Luisa jumping about the stage.)* Was she
   a U.F.O?

ALL: ¡Olvídarte!

LUISA: HA! HA! HA! HA!

*(She runs off-stage. We hear glass shattering and a loud
   "Ugh." Diane, Armando, Rick do a double take.)*

RICK: Calvino de Kline's "Obnoxious"...at K-Mart.

ALL: HA! HA! HA! HA!

Black Out.

Mexican American

RICK: *(Rick enters.)* I love commercials. They are so educa-
   tional. They let me know what I need. I got a lot of needs
   'cause I'm Mexican-American. Not just Mexican, but
   American needs. My American side needs football. My
   Mexican side needs bullfights....I know, its very violent
   and barbaric, but I love football. I need Mexican food. And
   American food. My Mexican side needs *carne asada.* My
   American side needs New York steak, which is basically
   bland *carne asada.* I love Mexican food. When I see that
   Rosarita Refried Bean commercial, my Mexican side just
   wants to take that Rosarita woman and put her on a
   kitchen table and, wango, wango, wango! and have twelve
   children through her. But my American side would like to
   get to know her better, talk to her, establish some hon-

esty, communication, and then wango, wango, wango!
And have 2.5 kids with her. My American side would like
to hang out with his friends, and that's called a fraternity.
But when my Mexican side hangs out with his friends, it's
called a street gang! I hate contradictions. I need a world
with no contradictions. We all need a world with no contradictions. I call myself Mexican so I won't forget my
past, and American because that's what I am. When do I
get to call myself an American? When do I get to drive
past San Clemente and not get stopped by a guy in a
green uniform on top of my trunk looking for illegal
aliens. I'm going to say something very controversial. I
love *folklórico* dancing. I don't think it's boring at all.
Whenever I see a hat in front of me... *(A Mexican hat is
thrown in front of him.)* Gotta dance! *(Tries to dance but
can't.)* Oh, my God, I've lost my rhythm. My American
side is invading my central nervous system. *(In a Mexican
voice.)* "You colonizing bastards." *(In a yuppie tone.)* "Go
back to Mexico, dude." *(Mexican voice.)* "I didn't cross the
border. The border crossed me." *(Yuppie voice.)* You for-
eigner. *(Mexican voice.)* You Gringo. *(Yuppie voice.)* You
beaner. *(Mexican voice.)* You *Gavacho. (Yuppie voice.)* You
wetback. *(Mexican voice.)* Wetback? Nobody calls me a
wetback. I'll kill you. *(He chokes himself. Yuppie voice.)*
Help me, help me! The Mexican is going to kill me. Help,
help! Somebody call the border patrol!

Lights black out on Rick, struggling on the floor.

Las Comadres

*A neighborhood park. Two women enter from opposite sides of
the stage. They are struggling with their kids who are off-
stage attached to long ropes. Each is carrying a patch of
astroturf they place in front of them.*

LUPE: *(Calling off-stage.)* No, José! I don't want to play tug of war! It's too early in the morning!

DOLORES: Pepe! Pepe! If you're good, I'll give you another twenty feet.

BOTH: *Ay*, kids

LUPE: This neighborhood.

DOLORES: It's falling apart. *(The two women eye each other.)*

LUPE: *(Calling out.)* Tico! Tico! Tico! Where are you?

DOLORES: Is that your son?

LUPE: No, its my dog. I'm very worried about him. I know I shouldn't say this…God will punish me. Santo Padre. *(She crosses herself.)*

DOLORES: Go ahead, say it!

LUPE: Well, ever since *los* Koreans have taken over the neighborhood, I live in fear that Tico will never live to see two.

DOLORES: *Ay, mujer.* I know exactly what you mean. I know I shouldn't say it…God will punish me. *(She crosses herself.)* Santo Padre.

LUPE: Go ahead, say it!

DOLORES: Well, some Vietnamese moved in next door to my neighbors and, nearly a year later, their cat disappeared.

BOTH: Kitty chop suey! *(Dolores' rope goes straight up in the air.)*

DOLORES: Pepe! Get down from that tree! *(She yanks on the rope and a thud is heard.)* That's my son.

LUPE: *(Looking at the boy.)* Oh, good, at least he's getting up. My! He's got a lot of chest hair for a little boy.

DOLORES: *Ay, gracias.* He's eight. We have a lot of Spanish blood where we're from: San Pablo.

LUPE: Oh, you're from San Pablo? I'm from San Pablo!

DOLORES: *¡No!*

LUPE: *¡Sí!*

DOLORES: *¡No!*

LUPE: *¡Sí!*

DOLORES: ¡No!

LUPE: *¡Sí!*

BOTH: *¡Comadre! (They hug.)*

DOLORES: Don't you have a crazy cousin?...

LUPE: Yes, he died.

BOTH: *Qué lástima.*

LUPE: You have a *Tía* María... the one with the really heavy mustache?

DOLORES: Yes , she died, too.

BOTH: *Qué lástima.*

LUPE: *(Offering her hand.)* Lupe.

DOLORES: Dolores, it's so good to meet you.

LUPE: What a small world! Let's sit down, *mujer. (They sit on bench.)*

DOLORES: And it's getting smaller and smaller all the time! This is the only place left in the neighborhood where it's safe for Pepe to play!

LUPE: But it's only safe at the crack of dawn. I have to put the alarm on at 5:45 in the morning.

DOLORES: For me it's 5:15. I need the extra time to unbolt and unchain all the locks in the house.

LUPE: And all this just so we can get here before *los*...I shouldn't say it...God will punish me. *(They both cross themselves.)*

DOLORES: Say it!

LUPE: So we get here before *los* blacks take over the park. *(We hear loud rap music.)* Must be one left over from last night.

DOLORES: Oh, hi, Leroy, How's the gang? *(They watch him pass.) Ay, m'ija.* I don't even know who controls the block these days. I never know what colors to dress Pepe in!

LUPE: *La* Fifth and Main. Completely taken over by...I'm just going say it, and God will have to punish me.

DOLORES: Oh, go ahead, say it. *(They cross themselves.)*

LUPE: Completely taken over by those really dark Colombians. The neighborhood is going to pot.

DOLORES: Pot? I wish it were only pot! I have to walk by there to get to the overpriced Jewish Deli. I see them with the white powder, even the old grandmother with a pile of it on her kitchen table, sifting it out, mixing in milk and eggs, putting it in a pan, sticking it in the oven, plain as day! You know, they all belong to that Medellín Quartet!

LUPE: They should all be forced to live with Cubans the way I've been forced to live with Cubans, right across the street from me.

DOLORES: And me! My life is a living purgatory thinking that Pepe could marry a *Cubana*. They're all addicts, you know? They got to have it. Five or six times a day. The black, bitter kind.

LUPE: The black, bitter kind?

DOLORES: Coffee! *Cochina.* Coffee! That's what makes the Cubans so aggressive. Lupe, it's such a blessing to find someone to talk to, who understands.

LUPE: I know, I know. So how long has it been since you have been back to beloved Panama?

DOLORES: Panama? I wouldn't set foot in Panama!

LUPE: You're not from San Pablo, Panama?

DOLORES: No I'm from San Pablo, Costa Rica!

LUPE: Slut!

DOLORES: *¡Puta!* Panamanian trash! I should have known from your over-processed hair. That's no perm!

LUPE: You and your mulatto son. That African darkie!

DOLORES: *¡Desgraciada!*

LUPE: *¡Tu madre!*

DOLORES: *¡La tuya! (To her son off-stage.)* Ay, m'ijo, you're not that dark.

(Dolores and Lupe exit cursing at one another.)

Piñataphobia Therapy

Armando, Luisa and Diane are standing blindfolded. It appears as if they are standing in front of a firing squad.

ARMANDO: Let's just get this over with.

DIANE: I knew it would end like this.

LUISA: Are you sure you don't need a blindfold, Rick?

RICK: No, I need to face this one. *(A Piñata flies in.)* God. It's horrible. Give me a blindfold.

LUISA: I'm at my seventh birthday party...

ARMANDO: Seventh birthday party...

DIANE: Birthday...

RICK: Party.

LUISA: I'm in San Jose, Guatemala.

ARMANDO: San Jose, Colombia.

DIANE: San Jose, California.

RICK: San Diego. *(Or local city.)*

LUISA: Someone put a blindfold on me and a baseball bat in my hand and started twirling me around and around and around. I took my first swing and heard this horrible crunching sound.

ARMANDO: It wasn't the piñata I had struck, it was little María Díaz's mouth. There was blood splattered all over her blue crinoline dress. Her front tooth was hanging by a thread.

DIANE: It was a horrible sight. To this day, I can't erase the image from my mind...and every time I see her now, and she smiles at me...that gold tooth...the memory of that horrible party comes back to haunt me.

RICK: Needless to say I never got another birthday party. I could never say, hey, man, come to my house, I'm having a party.... *(Singing.)* ..."It's my party and I'll cry if I want to..."*(Rick dissolves into tears as they all join the song.)*

ALL: "Cry if I want to... Cry If I want to... You would cry too," if your piñata attacked you, uh huh huh huh huh!

Blackout.

The Mayan Defense League

LUCY VOICE OVER: *(In the dark.)* Hello, Hermana Petra? Oh, God. It's bad, it's really bad. I'm holding a bottle of peroxide here, and this time I swear I'm going to use it! I'm going to dye my hair blonde!!

VOICE OVER PETRA: No, don't do it! This sounds like a job for...*(Three Mayans appear, behind scrim, superhero style. They are all dressed as what can only be described as Mayan paramedics.)*

OBSIDIAN BUTTERFLY, JAGUAR AND SNAKE: The Mayan Defense League! 976-4 MDL! *(They discover Lucy Garce in her apartment unconscious with "White food": Wonder bread, Twinkies and potato chips strewn throughout the apartment. Lucy moans.)*

OBSIDIAN: Let's get to work, Mayans.

BOTH MEN: Let's go, Mayans

JAGUAR: *(Picking up bottle.)* Peroxide! We're too late.

OBSIDIAN: *(Feeling for a pulse.)* No. We're not too late.

SNAKE: It was just a cry for help... Flatline! Pumping. *(Administering CPR.)*

OBSIDIAN: Check eyes.

JAGUAR AND SNAKE: No eyes.

OBSIDIAN: Walk her. *(She picks up a Twinkie.)* Oh, no. White food. Finger. Stand clear. *(She gags Lucy with her finger.)*

JAGUAR AND SNAKE: Standing clear!

LUCY: Who are you? What are you doing?

JAGUAR: Calm down. We are here to help you.

SNAKE: We've been sent to deprogram you. We're the M.D.L.

ALL: Mayan Defense League. 976-4 MDL.

JAGUAR: Snake Breath, check the apartment for toxins.

SNAKE: Right away, Jaguar Lips.

OBSIDIAN: *(To Lucy.)* All right, all right, don't you worry about a thing. You're going to be okay.

LUCY: No, you've got the wrong person. You've made a terrible mistake. You've got to believe me. I was just having a little anxiety attack. *(She pushes Obsidian and tries to escape.)* Help me! Someone help me!

SNAKE: (RUNNING IN) Obsidian Butterfly, we found one thousand frozen Jenny Craig dinners in the refrigerator!

JAGUAR: *(Out of breath.)* I found a life-size black velvet painting of Christie Brinkley!

OBSIDIAN: Get real, García. Your mind has been kidnapped and we're here to rescue it.

LUCY: How'd you know that was my real name?

OBSIDIAN: We found your old green card.

LUCY: Well it's not my real name. It's Lucy Garce.

OBSIDIAN: Oh really, come on, you expect me to believe that? What's your real name?

LUCY: It's Lucy Garce.

OBSIDIAN: What is it?

LUCY: It's Lucy Garce, damnit!

OBSIDIAN: You're a tough nut to crack, cookie, but I'm a nut cracker. *(Cracks her knuckles.)*

SNAKE AND JAGUAR: *(Running in.)* Oh, my God!

OBSIDIAN: What?!

SNAKE AND JAGUAR: Oh, my God!

OBSIDIAN AND LUCY: What?!

SNAKE AND JAGUAR: Blue contact lenses.

LUCY: What?! *(Lucy screams and tries to grab contact lenses from Jaguar Lips and Snake Breath. She fails.)*

OBSIDIAN: García, García, García. *(Obsidian, Jaguar and Snake conference.)*

JAGUAR: Fellow Mayans, it looks like we are going to have to use "The Procedure."

MAYANS: *"El* Procedure." *(Forming an assembly line.)*

OBSIDIAN: Tortilla.

JAGUAR: Tortilla.

SNAKE: Tortilla, García. Give me your hand. *(He slaps a tortilla into Lucy's hand.)* What does that look like? Feel good?

LUCY: Good...

OBSIDIAN: Smell like home?

LUCY: *(Gagging.)* Yeah... *(She tosses it behind her back.)*

OBSIDIAN: White bread.

JAGUAR: White bread.

SNAKE: White bread. *(He slaps a piece of white bread into Lucy's hand.)* What does that feel like?

LUCY: Oh, it's white.

SNAKE: Yes?...

LUCY: It's ever so white. White, lily snowy white! So white! I've got to have a bite. *(She stuffs it in her mouth.)*

ALL: *(Violently hitting her on the back.)* Spit it out! Spit it out! Spit it out!

LUCY: It was just a little piece of white bread!

SNAKE: Only a little piece of white bread? That's how it starts, García. Just a little piece of white bread. Just say no.

OBSIDIAN AND JAGUAR: Yes!

SNAKE: Fellow Mayans, I've never seen anyone suffering from such full-blown Latin Denialitis.

OBSIDIAN AND JAGUAR: Very bad!

SNAKE: It looks like we might have to resort to surgery.

JAGUAR: A triple cultural bypass.

OBSIDIAN: A Ritual-Otomy!

ALL: A Ritual- Otomy!

SNAKE: Obsidian Butterfly... prepare the tranquilizer. *(Obsidian begins to play a flute as Lucy goes into a trance. The others in Don Mayan garb to begin the ritual.)*

SNAKE: Yucatan! Mazatlan! Chaka Khan! Dayo, Dayo. *(Singing.)* Daylight come and I want to go home....

Dance, Mayans, dance! Dance your Mayan *nalgas* off.
(Obsidian and Jaguar do dance and intone Aztec chant.)
JAGUAR: Mayan's. We have work to do. *(All chant "Om.")*
ALL: Ommm. Ommm. Ommm. *(They turn to audience.)* Anglos, don't try this at home. Ommm.
LUCY: *(She starts regressing.)* Lucy Garce. Lucy Garce. *(With great effort.)* Lucí-a Garcí-a Lucía García. *(Childlike.)* I was born in Guatemala. I sold gum in the streets. " *Chicle. Chicle.*" *(A la Norma Desmond.)* No, I was Dolores del Río, Dolores del Río. That's it. They call me La Adelita. *(Singing.)* *"La cucaracha, la cucaracha, ya no puede caminar...."* *(Seductively.)* Cortez, *querido.* I will show you the way. Your Malinche will show you the way. *(Imperial.)* I was a Mayan Princess. I'm royalty... an illustrious turquoise.... Power... Blood... Sacrifice!!...*(She is possessed. She starts strangling Snake Breath. Jaguar Lips manages to subdue her with the Spock grab to her neck. She falls to the floor in a dead faint.)*
JAGUAR: Hey, that Vulcan thing really works. *(To Snake.)* You okay?
SNAKE: She turned Aztec on us. Cultural overdose.
JAGUAR: Twinkie. Stat!
OBSIDIAN: Twinkie. Stat. *(She shoves a Twinkie in Lucy's mouth.)* Stand and deliver her. Lucía García, you don't have to be a Mayan Princess or anyone special. Who you are is good enough.
LUCY: Who I am is good enough.
JAGUAR: Lucía García, just... *(Jaguar's beeper goes off.)* Looks like we have an emergency. In Beverly Hills. Better hurry.
OBSIDIAN: Who is it this time?
JAGUAR: Some guy named Charlie Sheen.
OBSIDIAN: Oh, yea. We helped his brother last week...Emilio. Let's pack it up.
SNAKE: A Mayan is a terrible thing to waste.

ALL: Lucía García! Just be who you are! Just be who you are! 976-4 MDL! *(They exit. Lucy is left on stage. She picks up a conch shell, which has been left behind. She gently blows it.)*

The lights slowly fade.

Final Meeting

(A rythmic, Latin version of "Pachelbel Canon in D" plays as Luisa, Rick, Diane and Armando walk on stage and form a line. Luisa holds the conch shell from the previous scene.

RICK: Hi, my name is Rick. I'm a Mexican-American, leaning more towards Mexican *un día* at a time.

DIANE: Hi, my name is Diane. And I'm a recovering Chicana.

ARMANDO: Hi, my name is Armando. And I'm a sensitive guy trapped in a macho body.

LUISA: Hi, my name is Luisa. And I admit I'm a Latina. *(Music swells.)*

Curtain.

Group Biography

Latins Anonymous was founded in 1987 by Luisa
Leschin, Armando Molina, Rick Nájera, and Diane Rodríguez.
Cristobal Franco, with his unique brand of humor, joined the
group in 1992. Mirroring the culture, they are very distinct
Latinos from diverse backgrounds. Luisa Leschin, the daugh-
ter of a concert pianist and El Salvadorian politician, was
raised in Guatemala and schooled in Europe and New York
City. Armando Molina's parents brought their family to the
United States from Colombia when Armando was 1-1/2 years
old and settled in Queens, New York. The Francos left Mexico
City and settled into the bland, blonde, middle class life of the
San Fernando Valley. Rick Nájera was born and raised in San
Diego and grew up living on the hyphen, dealing with being
Mexican and American. And Diane Rodríguez, a Chicana, is
the product of a performing family of ministers and singers
from San Jose, California, via Texas and the fields of California. Together Latins Anonymous forms a voice that addresses
the diversity of the Latino experience in the U.S. today.

Their signature play, *Latins Anonymous,* has received
eleven successful regional theater productions all over the
United States and abroad, at such theaters as South Coast

Repertory, San Diego Repertory, Borderlands (Arizona), Group Theater (Seattle), New World Theater (Amherst), and Guadalajara, Mexico. The play secured them their first pilot deal with ABC and a *Drama-logue* Award for best ensemble.

Their second play, *The La La Awards,* is a hilarious send up of T.V. award shows and current pop culture. It has received productions at the Japan American Center, The San Diego Repertory and The Guadalupe Cultural Arts Center, enjoying excellent reviews along the way.

Latins Anonymous, the group, has always enjoyed a reputation for trailblazing, and they continue to do so. Diane Rodríguez is co-Artistic Director of the Latino Theatre Initiative at the Tony award-winning theatre, the Mark Taper Forum. She continues to publish, direct and write. Her new play is the *Ballad of Ginger Esparza* commissioned by the Mark Taper Forum. Cris Franco is currently one of the head writers for Edward James Olmos Productions at ABC and his work on PBS' *The Puzzle Place* garnered that show a 1997 Emmy nomination and, for him, a 1997 Imagen Award. Señor Franco has finished penning his first comedy feature film, *Wooley Bully,* and his first one-man show, *The Mexican American Wars.* Luisa Leschin's comedy-writing talents have naturally led to sit-com. She has just completed a Disney Studios Writing Fellowship during which time she wrote scripts for *Frasier, Ellen, 3rd Rock From the Sun and Cybil.* Rick Nájera was named one of the 50 People to Watch in Hollywood by *Weekly Variety.* He is currently developing a Showtime series and co-created the series *The American Family* for UPN. Armando Molina is a member of the Cornerstone Co., which is dedicated to bringing theatre to inner city communities, and is a founding member of the Platform, a political cabaret. Señor Molina is co-author of the avant-garde comic re-mix of the film, *El Luchador Chicano,* and has been commissioned to write for the Getty Research Institute and the Virginia Avenue Project. They all continue to act on stages, in front of cameras and on therapists' couches.

Muchas gracias to the following theater companies, actors and directors who have helped make *Latins Anonymous* the most produced Latino play in the United States:

San Diego Repertory Theater, San Diego, CA (6/1/90 to 8/5/90). Directed by Miguel Delgado, featuring the original cast

Seattle Group Theatre, Seattle, WA (5/30/91 to 6/21/91). Directed by Luisa Leschin, featuring Julia Calderon, Richard Cansino, Julie Chavez, Albert Michael

Borderlands Theatre, Tucson, AZ (3/12/92 to 3/22/92 and 7/3/92 to 7/23/92). Directed by Diane Rodriguez, featuring Roberto Garcia, Norma Medina, Richard Trujillo, and Alida Wilson-Gunn

Actors Lab, Scottsdale, AZ (2/12/92 to 3/8/92). Directed by Jan Rothman Sickler, featuring Norma Medina, Roberto Garcia, Syndia Fontes, Nick Glaser, and Zarco

Sacramento Theatre Co., Sacramento, CA (3/92). Directed by Rick Najera, featuring Julia la Riva, Anne Betancourt, Gustavo Ruelas, and Robert Covarrubias

South Coast Repertory, Costa Mesa, CA (5/18/92 to 6/5/92). Directed by Miguel Delgado, featuring Julia la Riva, Armando Molina, Rick Najera, and Diane Rodriguez

LA Teatro and 7/11 Unlimited Theatre, Department of Theatre Arts & Dance, California State University, Los Angeles, CA (4/1/93 to 4/10/93). Directed by Gabriel Enriquez, featuring Edna Alvarez, Mily Escalante, Victor Duran, and Paul G. Saucido

The America Southwest Theatre Company in association with New Mexico State University, NM (3/95). Directed by Armando Molina, featuring Linda Sandoval, Andreas López, Jos Viramontes, Lora Martínez-Cunningham